For I Know
the Plans

Bailey Bowers

Bailey
Bowers ♡

Jer. 29:11-13

ISBN 978-1494938666
Tile ID 4608646

Printed in the United States of America

This book is dedicated to Paige Elizabeth Kriegel.
Paige taught me so much in her twenty years,
more than anyone else has ever taught me,
she invested so much of her life in me.
She still is like a sister to me, a best friend.
She went to be with Jesus on Tuesday July 24th,
2012, and we miss her terribly.
But in her honor I publish this book, so that she will
always be remembered by those who love her.

Paige, I will never forget you, dear friend.
Thank you for everything you taught me.
I miss you more than you can imagine,
I will always, always love you.

Romans 8:37-39

"No, in all these things we are more than conquerors through him who loved us. For I am sure that neither death nor life, nor angels nor rulers, nor things present nor things to come, nor powers, nor height nor depth, nor anything else in all creation, will be able to separate us from the love of God in Christ Jesus our Lord."

Prologue

"Chrissy, watch out!" Carter shouted as he threw himself across me; guarding my body with his own. My head started to spin as I tried to gain control of the car. It was useless. We spun in circles and suddenly everything went black and a sharp pain ran through my head. The next thing I heard were sirens and unfamiliar voices shouting words I couldn't comprehend.

Where am I? What's going on?

"Chrissy, can you hear me?" someone asked.

I just nodded as I slowly opened my eyes. My head pounded.

"Does anything hurt?" the same voice questioned.

"Just my head," was all I could respond without feeling dizzy.

"You were unconscious for a few minutes but you will be able to think clearly in just a little while." I took in my surroundings. Frantically searching the ambulance I could not find Carter. Panic filled my chest and I reminded myself to keep breathing.

"Where's my brother? Is he okay?" I asked frantically. Things started to make sense. It was all coming back to me. The instantaneous shattering of my car, Carter leaning over to guard my body, excruciating pain striking my forehead as it hit the steering wheel and I lost control of the vehicle.

"He's hurt, but he will be okay. We think he broke his leg, maybe his foot, but we aren't sure. We are on our way to the hospital. " My face felt hot and wet. I reached my hand up to feel my cheek. It came away wet but not with the blood as I feared it would, only with the tears I was unconsciously crying. As they continued streaming down my face my thoughts began to clarify and I wondered, *why did this have to happen?*

The whole way to the hospital all I could think about was how excited I had been just two weeks ago for Carter's return from Uganda. This was supposed to be a time of refreshment. It was meant to be a summer filled with long days at the pool, my best friends, and a trip to New York. And now, I had no idea what was going to happen.

Chapter 1

I looked out the car window, counting each exit we passed on the highway. Feeling my heart pounding in my chest, I thought through all that had happened within the last two years.

My twenty-four year old brother Carter had left to go to Uganda through an international mission organization. Carly, my older sister, had finished her sophomore year at Gardner-Webb and had started her junior year. I thought about all the days before Carter left for Uganda and could picture myself watching him board the plane the day he left. I saw all the days he would take me to get ice cream when I had had a bad day. Stuck in my mind was the memory of the day he got his license and we rode all over our small town together. With each little diner, café, and local shop we passed downtown there was someone new to wave to. When we were younger, he didn't mind playing games or watching movies with me even though I'm sure he had much better things he could have been doing. Most of the time Carter was the one I talked to about everything: my problems, my struggles, and my joys. He was always there to talk, always had the right thing to say and that's what meant the most.

I thought through the emails he sent me about the guest house, about the orphanage, about Rob and Amber, the couple from church he worked with. He was finally coming home for a month. After two years in Uganda, he would be home again! It had been a long two years.

As we got off the exit, my heart beat faster.

"Dad, unlock the doors, hurry!" I shouted as we pulled into the airport parking lot.

"Calm down! I've got to park first. Someone excited to see their big brother, huh?" He unlocked the doors and I hurried out of the car into the airport. I checked my phone and saw that his plane had landed early. He should have been making his way through security by now, maybe even getting his luggage. Checking my phone again I searched through the sea of faces for Carter.

At last I saw him and tears welled in my eyes as I finally found and recognized the familiar face smiling in my direction. He was just coming through the baggage claim. I bolted across the room and into his arms; his strong, welcoming, comforting arms. A few of my tears stained his shirt and I stood speechless, breathing in his familiar scent. Things felt a bit more normal for a few seconds before my parents came to join our hug. When we all stepped back I noticed his caramel blonde hair was

longer, his dark eyes were brighter and his once smooth
cheeks were covered in stubble.

Our local airport was filled with the sounds of
families greeting their brothers and sisters, and sons and
daughters welcoming their parents. "We've missed you
so much. How was your flight, and your trip?" my mom
yelled above the noise as she stood with her arm around
her oldest son.

"My flight was long, but Uganda was incredible, I
felt at home so quickly. I have so many stories to tell you
guys but I'm going to need something to eat, airplane
food can't hold you over for long."

"What do you want?" I asked as we walked out of the
airport, and with his arm around my shoulder, we hopped
into the car.

"A burger!" he said decidedly.

"Sounds good," Dad agreed as he drove us towards
town.

"I can't believe how you've changed," mom
commented, "You look so much older."

Carter and I laughed in the backseat.

"You say that when I've only been gone a day,
mom," he jokingly responded though it was completely
true.

"What did you miss the most while you were gone?"
I asked him, secretly hoping it would be our brother-sister
dates.

"Well, I missed you guys of course. If we're talking
material things I'd have to say your caramel cookie

brownies, mom. When one of the kids in the villages asked what heaven was like I tried describing them but I didn't do them justice. "

Mom laughed and asked, "What are you going to miss most about Uganda while you're here?"

"I think I'll just miss the people and the incredible opportunities God gave us to serve each and every day. He definitely gives us those here but it's so evident over there.

"Speaking of awesome opportunities, when I go back in a month, we're going to begin working with an organization called Sole Hope. They go into villages and schools and remove jiggers from children's feet. I know I've probably mentioned it before but jiggers are a sand flea that burrow into the people's feet and have to be removed with a sharp object like a safety pin or a razor blade. The jiggers are more common in children but they are extremely painful. If they can get shoes, the problem can be easily solved. If they don't get shoes and the jiggers aren't removed they can spread up their body. If it gets bad enough it can even paralyze them. One of the worst cases we saw was a young girl named Joy with jiggers covering her feet and her fingers. It was heartbreaking.

"We're going to use the orphanage as a place to host jigger clinics for several weeks where people can come for help since it's such a central location in the city. It's going to be a lot of work and something new for all of us, but in the end it will be worth it! It's been something we've been planning for a really long time." With each new sentence his love for this country and these people became more evident. The way he spoke showed how much he had been moved by his experiences and how he longed to be back. I couldn't help but be enthralled with everything he said, it seemed so much more interesting than my life had ever been.

"How long will this last?" I asked.

"Well, it will only be in the mornings from about eight to one and it's going to last about a month. If it goes really well this time, we might do it again later and even go with them to some other villages."

"I'm so proud of all God has used you to do and I know He's going to continue doing amazing things," Mom said her face glowing with pride.

"That's just what we're praying for. I have to tell you about this family who came to Dru and Asher, the people who run Sole Hope. There were four kids, the oldest was only seven. Dad was out of the picture as in most homes in Uganda. The grandmother was the primary caretaker because the mom was so sick and part of her sickness was due to jiggers. One day the oldest two children along with their grandmother came to Dru and Asher because they had heard what they had been doing to help people with jiggers. They were desperate for help. As it turns out, all of the children and the grandmother had severe cases but nothing like their mom's.

"Dru and Asher asked me to go with them to this family's home when they went to visit her. When we got there the youngest child, barely a year old, was crying, and the mother just couldn't get to sleep. This was one of the first times I had been out into the villages and the situations of these people continued to shock me. You wouldn't believe it. I'll have to show you the picture of their house when we get home.

"Anyway, the grandmother woke the mother up so they could begin working on her feet. While I helped one of the Sole Hope nurses work on the children's feet, a look of fear came over the mother when she saw the needles near her feet. Dru and Asher ended up bringing the entire family back to the Sole Hope guest house so the mother could get further care and the grandmother could be educated on how to remove the jiggers. That's just one of the many cases they've dealt with like that. It's so hard to accept that as reality for these people."

"I can't imagine," Mom said with tears brimming.

Once we got home, Carter and I headed up to his room to unpack some of his stuff.

"So has it been weird with me and Carly both gone?" Carter asked me as I continued unloading things from his suitcase for him to put away. He had already taken his clothes downstairs for Mom to wash and all that was left in his bags were souvenirs and gifts.

"You have no idea," I responded, "It just gets so lonely."

"I bet," Carter started as I pulled out a pair of multi-colored soft cotton pants.

"What are these?" I asked giggling while I held up the pants in front of me. He was just coming back from putting something away in the bathroom.

He laughed, "I actually got those for you. It's not your only gift but everyone says they're super comfortable. I know they look crazy but I thought they might be good homework pants."

"The more I look at them the more I like them actually!" We laughed together.

Oh how I've missed this. I thought to myself when I heard Mom yell at Carter from downstairs, "Carter!" she exclaimed, "I made your favorite caramel cookie brownies!"

"Okay, be down in a minute!" We put away a few more things and Carter grabbed his laptop off of his bed before we went downstairs. Mom was bustling back and forth, washing mounds of laundry covered with the aroma of the Ugandan streets, and finishing up Carter's brownies along with some of his other favorite goodies.

"Mom, I want to show you and Dad my pictures!" Carter said as she walked by carrying a basket of clothes.

"Okay, be there in a minute," Mom said as she turned the oven off. We all gathered around in curiosity awaiting the stories Carter had to tell. Mom came in and sat a towering plate of brownies on the coffee table along with a pitcher of sweet tea. Carter plugged his laptop up to the TV and began clicking through his hundreds of pictures.

13

"So, this picture is of the guest house that Rob and Amber run. We don't spend a whole lot of time here each day, only in the mornings and after dinner."

"Wow! It's nicer than I thought," I commented after seeing the guest house. It was a two-story brick home. The front porch looked more than welcoming with its white swing and purple flowers.

"This one is the orphanage that we work with. Usually before lunch, when it's not unbearably hot, we work on church planting, and then after lunch we work in the orphanage. "

"How many children do they have there?" I asked after seeing some of the pictures of the orphanage.

"Over a hundred, at least. They have kids from birth to age five."

"In that small of a space?" I couldn't picture that many kids in such a cramped place.

"Yeah, their lives aren't easy."

The pictures showed a building that looked like it was falling apart. The bricks that had to have been put together many years ago were now chipped on the edges and the paint on the doors had faded long ago. In front of this building was a gate, a giant blue gate and like the doors the paint was peeling. The fence on each side of the gate was taller than the buildings and barbed wire and shards of glass lined the top keeping intruders away. Inside each child was wearing tattered clothes but their faces somehow managed a smile for the camera.

"You all are part of the church planting program, right?" I asked, trying to get this picture out of my head.

"Yep. We have found that by serving in the orphanage, and meeting the physical needs of people around Jinja they become more acceptable of the gospel we want to teach them about.

"And here's that family I was telling you about."

In the picture was a family of six, none of them smiling with the exception of the three year old little boy. They stood in front of a one room shack made of mud, sticks and straw surrounded by huts just the same as theirs.

"Is that their house?" Mom asked, "No wonder the mom was so sick, with all those people in such a small space it's a wonder she could ever rest."

Carter simply nodded, "This was just two weeks later at the Sole Hope guest house." Clicking to the next picture we saw the same family. Dressed in clean clothes with shoes on their feet, they were all smiling. Their faces now exuded joy.

"Love makes all the difference in the world," Mom said smiling at the picture on the screen.

"Yeah, and new shoes!" I replied and we all laughed.

By 10:00 we had seen all of his pictures and videos. Even though it went on for hours, each new story accompanied by pictures captivated me even more, giving me a more complete picture of this place Carter had fallen in love with. While getting ready for bed I stood pulling my hair up into a messy bun in front of my floor length mirror. As I stood there I noticed my closet door standing wide open. There hung an overabundance of clothes and dozens of pairs of shoes. My eyes were stuck on the flowery sandals and flowy sundresses but transfixed in my mind were the Ugandan babies in Carter's pictures who were barely clothed and with no shoes. I closed my eyes and purposefully thought of something else, *Hunter. I haven't heard from him today.* I settled down on my bed to call my boyfriend.

"Hey," he said.

"Hey Hunter."

"Why didn't you answer my calls earlier?" He asked me curiously and quickly answered his own question, "Right! Carter came home from Uganda today."

Though he sounded exhausted, I was glad he remembered. After all, I had just told him the night before. Sometimes he tended to be a bit forgetful.

"How's he doing?"

"Great, but really tired. He's already shared so many stories with us. He just showed Mom, Dad, and me all of his pictures and videos. It took almost two hours!"

I could imagine the bewildered look on his face as he asked, "How many pictures did he have?"

"Hundreds. But I've had enough of Uganda. How are you? You sound pretty worn out."

"I'm all right, it's been a long day."

"I'm sorry. What happened? Have your parents been fighting again?"

"Of course. It's gotten really bad these last couple of days but now my dad is saying he wants to leave. I don't see how things could get much worse before they completely fall apart."

"I'm so sorry. I can't imagine how you feel, how all of you feel."

"Can we just not talk about it right now? I need a break from all of that."

"Absolutely."

"So no more Uganda, no more of my parents." Again I heard the smile on his face.

"What about New York? Is that an acceptable topic?" I paused before saying anything else and put my hand over the speaker, as Carter peeked his head in the door.

"Can we talk?" Carter asked.

"Sure, just a sec," I said to Carter, and then to Hunter, "Hey, can I call you later?"

"Sure, bye."

"Bye."

"Love you!" he said.

"Love you, too." We both hung up and Carter walked in.

"So what did you want to talk about?" I asked as he sat down in my desk chair on the opposite side of the room.

"Nothing in particular. I've been talking all about me. Let's talk about you."

17

"Okay. Well, where to start?"

"How about school?" We started talking, first school, then friends, then things going on at home. Occasionally he would throw in some much-needed advice. While we talked I realized how much I had really missed him. We talked over skype and emailed all the time but it just wasn't the same as sitting across the room from him.

Then he brought up something I could just tell would be awkward. Church. We go to church. I'm a Christian, but ever since Carter had left for Africa two years before I just hadn't been as serious about reading my Bible, or praying, or surrounding myself with godly influences. He was the one who always encouraged me to do those things. Honestly, Carter was always encouraging the whole family to go to church and to be involved. When he left for college things began to slowly slip and then after Carly left it got even worse.

"How is church?"

"Fine, I guess."

"Just fine? You used to love it." As he responded a look of concern covered his face.

"I know, I guess things are different now."

"How different? God is still God, he's not going to change, Chrissy." He paused. I didn't say anything because I knew I was guilty and he didn't speak because I knew he didn't want to offend me on his first night home.

Moments later he continued, "Are you still dating that guy? Oh, what was his name?" With this he came and sat beside me on my bed, looking right into my eyes.

"Hunter, and yes. I don't know, it's just been harder with you gone, I guess I haven't been as focused." I picked up a blanket at the end of my bed and slowly folded it, keeping busy as long as possible. For the two years Carter had been gone, Hunter and I had been either dating or really close friends. I didn't mention Hunter to him a whole lot, maybe because he's my big brother and he's protective and maybe because he doesn't want to see me get hurt. The topic never really came around. Okay, I guess I never let it come around.

"Is he helping with that?"

"Hunter? Helping with what?" My mind shot in all different directions trying to avoid this conversation at all costs.

"Is he helping you stay focused, or is he distracting you from growing?"

"You know, it's been a long day for you. You probably need to get some rest." I refolded the same pink blanket, not making eye contact, and wondering if the blanket matched the heat I felt in my face. To distract him, and hoping to change the subject, I threw one of my many frilly throw pillows at him as he stood up.

"Don't change the subject," he said throwing the pillow back at me and he walked out, "We will talk later, okay?"

"Okay," I said. He peeked his head back in, he added, "I've missed you, Chrissy."

"Missed you more, I'm so glad you're home." He walked back in, kissed me on the forehead and walked out saying, "I am too, love you!"

"Love you, too," I replied and fell asleep quickly after a long but very good day.

Chapter 2

"Morning Mom, morning Dad. Where's Carter?" I asked as I walked down the brown carpeted steps of our two-story house into the kitchen at 7:45 the next morning. Mom and Dad were sitting together at the table eating oatmeal. While eating Dad read the paper and Mom was looking at something on her phone.

"He's in his room, getting ready for church," my mom replied.

"Oh." I sat down across from her at the table, the conversation Carter and I had the night before replaying in my mind. Mom and Dad continued to talk but I was busy in my own thoughts. *Please don't let him come down here now. I really don't want to have this conversation right now, much less in front of the whole family.*

"Are you going to go with us?" Dad asked, folding his newspaper into quarters. His question startled me and brought me out of my thoughts.

"You guys are going?" I asked looking up at him with wide eyes. I couldn't remember the last time we had been to church together as a family.

"Yes, we are. I know we haven't been very consistent lately about going to church but with Carter being home we really need to make an effort to be there on a regular basis. I don't want to disappoint him," Mom said nodding her head, "Plus, it's the right thing to do."

"Okay," I said as I turned around and walked right back up the steps to take a quick shower. Once I got out, I pulled a cute knee-length sundress over my head and slipped my favorite Rainbow sandals on my feet. Standing as tall as my five-six frame would let me, I smoothed my dress out in front of the mirror and grabbed my makeup from the bathroom. My deep brown, curly locks fell off of my shoulders, their waves wet and unkempt from the shower. As I ran the mascara brush over my long eyelashes, the black of the liquid accentuated the blue of my eyes. After making sure my foundation had covered up all of the blemishes on my cheeks, I hurried back downstairs to grab something for breakfast.

"So, you're going with us?" Carter asked as he inhaled Mom's oatmeal and sausage that he hadn't seen in two years.

"Yep."

"Good. You look really pretty, by the way."

"Thanks, I would say you look pretty too but that would be weird, so you look nice."

"Thanks," he said laughing.

"You shaved!" I jokingly stated, scooping my oatmeal into a bowl.

"I'm glad you noticed," he laughed, "It feels a little strange to be honest."

I smiled and poured myself a glass of juice before sitting down beside him at the bar.

"Hey," he put down his spoon and looked right at me, "So about that conversation we were about to have last night."

"What about it?" I knew exactly where he was going with this. It was what I had been dreading all morning. My stomach churned and the bite of oatmeal in my mouth seemed to grow.

"I'm just worried about you. Now that we're together I just want to make sure you're at a healthy place," he was interrupted by Mom talking from the top of the steps.

"We need to leave in twenty minutes, you two better hurry!" She said louder than I expected.

"I better go fix my hair." I acted on her comment quickly, even if it was just to avoid this conversation.

"You didn't even finish your breakfast!" Carter said with a sigh as I ran down the hallway.

"Chrissy!" Mom yelled a few minutes later while I was putting the last bit of product in my thick hair.

"What?" I yelled back.

"We need to go!"

"Okay." I gasped as I saw what time it was. I made sure each thick, natural curl was in place before giving one last spritz of hairspray. As I made my way back downstairs I remembered something, *my Bible!* I ran back to my room and grabbed it from the shelf underneath my nightstand where it had sat undisturbed for weeks.

"You ready?" Dad asked as I ran downstairs.

"Yep." We walked out the door and he locked it behind us all.

"Gross!" I exclaimed as I stepped in the sopping wet, muddy yard, "Clearly it rained last night."

"Yeah, did you not hear it?" Carter asked as he laughed.

"No! Now my shoes are disgusting," I said under my breath.

"Just get in the car, it will be okay," Dad was getting impatient, so I quickly climbed in the car, careful not to step into any more mud. Now my feet (and favorite sandals!) were filthy, Dad was frustrated because we were on the verge of being late and honestly there was nothing in me that wanted to go to church. This was not going to be a very good morning.

When we got there I stepped out of the car and straightened my dress as we walked inside, trying to ignore the fact that the mud on my feet was squishing between my toes.

"Mom, I'm going to the bathroom," I told her. Hopefully I could dry my feet off a bit. I had nothing to work with except paper towels and soap but I did the best I could.

I came out to the sight of the rest of the family in mid conversation with our pastor. "How was Uganda?" he asked Carter, giving him a warm welcome back.

"It was incredible, but it's great being back home. I have so many amazing stories to tell you guys. How are you doing? How are the kids?"

"I'm doing just fine and they are great. You wouldn't believe how much they've grown. Katie is dancing and Josh and Jackson are playing on the spring tee-ball team, you'll have to come to one of their games while you're home."

"I'd love to," Carter replied with a smile. When Carter was in the youth ministry, the current pastor was the youth minister and he hung out at their house all the time. Their three kids adored him, especially the twin boys.

"I'll call you this week, I'd love to have lunch and catch up. We need to set up a time for you to speak to the congregation."

"Sounds great! See you this week, then." Carter shook his hand and we made our way into the service. I stood with everyone else as they sang a few songs that somehow I still seemed to know by heart but didn't feel like singing. The worship center was packed that morning. A couple hundred chairs were full of people joyful to be there. While our pastor spoke, I was distracted with thoughts of Hunter, my girlfriends, school, wanting a new pair of shoes... *maybe we can get pedicures this week!* I thought. Mom jabbed me with her elbow, "Open your Bible!" She whispered.

Her Bible was opened to Ephesians so I fumbled through the pages of my Bible until I came to the right passage and tried to stay focused on the rest of the sermon.

"Mom, are we staying for Sunday school?" I whispered to her during the last part of the service desperately hoping the answer was no.

"Yes," she responded with agitation. This was going to be weird, I had not gone to church in weeks, and it had been months since I had attended Sunday school! Without Carter even my parents didn't feel the same connection to our church.

"Chrissy! Where have you been?" my Sunday school teacher, Natalie, asked, coming up to hug me downstairs in the basement youth area.

"Hey. I've just been really busy," I lied, knowing I just didn't make it a priority to be there.

"I saw Carter in the service this morning! When did he come home?" She inquired as we walked towards our eleventh grade classroom.

"He came back yesterday, actually."

"I bet you're glad he is home. What kind of stuff was he doing there?"

"He was working with Rob and Amber Johnson in church planting work. They also worked in orphanages almost every day as well."

"That's awesome, I know you missed him. Does he go back?"

"He does, in about a month." We walked into my class, and I was welcomed by everybody like I'd been gone for years. As I sat in Sunday school, I listened to the conversation they were having. Apparently there was a senior class mission trip they were going on next summer.

"Chrissy," Natalie called on me after they had finished their conversation, "Why don't you tell us a little bit about what Carter is doing in Uganda?"

"Um," they all looked at me with imploring eyes, "Sure, I guess."

She nodded me on when I didn't begin at once.

"Well he's been working with Rob and Amber Johnson on church planting in different villages. They also frequently visit the orphanages in town. When he goes back in a month they'll be working with an organization called Sole Hope. They remove jiggers, which is a parasite, from people's feet and give them shoes," I stopped talking not knowing what else to say.

"Any questions?" Natalie asked looking around the room.

"Are you going to go visit him this summer?" one of the guys asked.

"I'm actually going to New York this summer, so probably not." *Why would I go visit him? That's completely out of the question.* I thought to myself.

"Thank you, Chrissy," Natalie gave me a warm smile and began her lesson. While she spoke I checked my phone at least every five minutes hoping to see a text from Hunter but the time seemed to crawl by. Finally the clock hit twelve o'clock. Time to leave. A pang of guilt hit my chest as I picked up my purse and made my way out of the classroom. I realized I should have enjoyed church, or at least have gotten something from it, but like I had told Carter it's just *different*.

I walked down the halls, recognizing a familiar face here and there, hoping to pass Carter on my way to the car.

"Did you guys go to your old class?" I asked Mom when I met her and Dad in the lobby on the way to the car.

"We did, it was great. How was Sunday school?" she asked in reply.

"Fine, what did you do during Sunday school hour, Carter?" he had just walked up after talking to someone else.

"I went to the college class. Next week they want me to give a report about Uganda and show some pictures. I had a few on my phone but they want to see more. It was really great getting to see everybody. There were a few people here for the weekend but we'll have more in the next couple weeks when people come home for the summer."

"That's cool. Mom, what are we doing for lunch?" I asked as we made our way to the car.

"We are going to meet your sister!"

"Really? When was this planned?" I was so excited to have the family together for just a few hours.

"A few weeks ago actually," Dad replied as he pulled out of the parking lot.

"Even I knew about it!" Carter chimed in with a smile.

"Why didn't I know?" I whined.

"We wanted to surprise you!" Carter announced.

After driving for an hour to get to a restaurant about an hour away from her school, I saw Carly's car in the parking lot. On the back of her car was the Gardner Webb bulldogs sticker and a Carolina Tar Heels symbol. Before banging on her window, I noticed she was doing something on her phone.

"BOO!" I shouted, and she jumped in her car, quickly slipping her phone into her pants pocket.

"Chrissy!" she shouted and got out of her car, giving me a big hug. I stepped back and Carter walked up. They stood hugging each other in the parking lot, tears pooling in her eyes. Finally our family was back together. I knew it wouldn't be for long, but we were together for just a little while and that's all I needed. I sat down between Carly and Carter at the table and the waiter took our drink orders.

"So, how's school?" Dad asked as our waiter walked away.

"It's good. I've got this project due at the end of the semester..." she kept talking and I couldn't help but think, *this is the perfect opportunity to snoop on her phone!* I reached quietly over into her lap and grabbed her phone. We had always told each other everything, I mean we're sisters after all, but I felt like she had been keeping something from me lately. It hit me at that moment that we hadn't really talked in at least a month.

It wasn't hard to break the code on her phone; she used the same password for everything. After unlocking her phone I saw her background but decided to wait a minute before questioning her since she and Dad were in the middle of a conversation. Who was this guy standing with his arm around her waist in the picture? I wanted to see what she had been looking at in her car so I turned straight to her texts. Yes, it seemed a little personal, but I wanted to know if she had been keeping something from me.

She had just deleted all of her old messages. That was like her, always keeping things neat and tidy. All were gone but the most recent which was sent to Nathan at one twenty-seven, exactly ten minutes ago. I had never heard her mention anyone named Nathan and certainly no one who deserved three hearts next to his name in her contact information. It was inquisition time.

"Who is this?" I whispered to her pointing at her background picture.

She glanced down at her lap and snatched the phone from my hand, "You took my phone! How did you know my password?"

"Please, you've used the same password for everything since you were seven."

She rolled her eyes at me.

"Now who is it?"

"Nobody." She gave me that look that said, *"Would you please not mention it!"*

"Oh really..."

"Carly, who is it?" my dad questioned after overhearing us. I couldn't wait to hear this.

When Carly was in high school she dated several guys who weren't the best influence on her. One was manipulative, another was rude not only to her but our entire family, another was a freshman in college when she was a sophomore in high school, which is never a good idea. After these relationships Carly made some drastic improvements in her life, shaping her to be a beautiful example for me. But even three years later, my dad still didn't really trust her in her discernment with boys. She had been blind to her own faults and her decisions hadn't exactly helped my efforts in dating either. As a result my dad didn't like either of us going out with guys, much less ones he had never met. Prime example: this Nathan guy.

"That's Nathan," she hesitantly replied.

"And," my mom wanted to know more.

"And, we've been dating for four months."

"Carly, you know we like to know the guys you and Chrissy date. Why did you keep it from us so long?" my dad began.

31

"We had just started talking at Christmas and I didn't want to make him feel uncomfortable right at the start by bringing him to meet you guys. We go to church and Bible study together. He loves Jesus and I told him all your rules. I just want to wait and let you meet him in person. I promise, next time I come home, he will come with me." Carter and I looked at each other and I knew we were thinking the same thing; *she is going to get it.* I also knew she didn't want the hassle of my dad asking her about her boyfriend every other day while she was away at college trying to have her own life.

"I don't like it, Carly," Dad said looking down at his menu, shaking his head, "I don't know anything about this guy: where he's from, who is family is, what he's like."

"His family lives about two hours away from Gardner-Webb in a pretty small city, it's where he grew up. Nevertheless, I'm sorry. I should have told you." Then the waiter came up and took our order, ending that conversation. I was crossing my fingers that the topic of my boyfriend didn't come up, but sure enough, she wanted to get revenge and just *had* to start questioning me. Not in girl time, but in front of the whole family.

"So, Chrissy, how's Hunter?"

"Actually, really good, thank you," then I leaned over and whispered to her, "Can't we talk about this later?"

"Actually no," she snapped back, "We had to talk about my boyfriend so now it's your turn." I looked at her again, pleading her to postpone this conversation.

"Fine," she said with a sigh, returning to search the menu for what she wanted to eat.

An hour later our food had been devoured but none of us were ready to leave quite yet. Dad ordered desert though none of us were hungry anymore. We were just getting used to being together again and wanted more time spent as a family. The laughter we shared increased by the moment and Carter had just finished telling Carly another story from Uganda when the waiter brought our caramel cheesecake.

Thirty minutes had passed when we realized we needed to get home. Walking Carly out to her car, we shared one last laugh about an old memory before giving our goodbye hugs.

"I'll be home soon and we'll talk about Hunter," she said as we stood hugging in the parking lot.

"Can't wait." I smiled as I said this but for some reason it was another conversation I didn't want to have. We waved goodbye as she drove off in her little red car.

Every moment of the drive back to the house Dad had some new opinion to share about Nathan; something else cynical to say.

"You know, Dad, maybe he's not a loser like the other guys she's dated," I threw out there trying to offer a positive comment in this situation.

"Maybe she's right, honey, he might be a really good guy," Mom added.

"I still just get so worried for her seeing where boys have taken her in the past. It's taken her a long time to get over that." Dad looked concerned as he spoke but changed the subject quickly, "You know Chrissy, I haven't seen Hunter in a while."

. All eyes were on me. *Really? Right now?* I thought.

"That's true, where has he been? I mean, I know he didn't hang out at the house a whole lot in the first place but," Mom joined in on Dad's commentary.

"But what?" I was trying to avoid having to be too brutally honest. In all reality, aside from school, I hadn't seen him that much either.

"All I'm saying is that maybe he should come over more often." Mom and Dad seemed to agree. Dad soon returned to the negative "what if's" and I breathed a sigh of relief. It only took ten more minutes of that to put me to sleep in the car.

That night I was sitting on my bed texting Hunter. All day I had been waiting for him to want to talk but it never came. Finally at ten o'clock my phone buzzed beside me on the bed. I guess I should say I sent him a message first but whatever.

"Chrissy," Carter peeked his head in the door.

"Hey." *Oh no, here it comes.* I thought for the second time that day.

"Can I come in?"

"Sure." He came in and plopped down on my bed with me.

"What are you doing?"

"Texting Hunter."

"Does he come around much? I mean, do ya'll hang out here at all? I was just wondering after what Mom said this afternoon."

"Sometimes." I put my phone down to really answer his question, "We usually go out to dinner or the movies and occasionally he comes here for dinner but we normally go out places."

"Oh okay. Well, you should see if he would want to come over one night while I'm home so I could get to know him."

"I'll ask him."

"When do you get out of school?" His mood lightened up a bit with this question.

"Two, we are done on May 27th, and then I'm free to spend the next couple weeks with you!"

"Good, I want us to have a day together once school is out. Okay?"

"I would love to."

"When does Carly get out?"

"I think next weekend. Can you believe she didn't tell Dad she had a boyfriend, she tells me everything!"

"Yeah, I totally thought she was going to get it from Dad. He was so mad."

"I know, it was hilarious!" We kept talking for a bit. Finally I kicked him out before the God conversation came up.

"Goodnight," I said to him as he walked out shutting the door quietly so Mom and Dad wouldn't hear. While I washed my face, my thoughts were everywhere but the main thing that kept occurring was the fact that I was hiding something from Carter. I knew he wasn't going to be happy about my shallow and inconsistent relationship with God. It didn't matter how uncomfortable the conversation would feel; between this and Hunter, it was the first thing I had purposefully not told him! And to be honest, it felt horrible.

Chapter 3

"Mom, I'm leaving. See you later." I whispered peeking my head in her door and quietly tip-toed down the steps as to not wake up Carter. Hunter was meeting me for breakfast before school. I hopped in my lime-green bug and drove away with music playing through the speakers.

"Hey, Chrissy." Hunter came up to me and grabbed my hand when I walked into our favorite local diner.

"Hey, did you get our food?"

"Sure did, a bacon, egg, and cheese biscuit for me, a fresh blueberry muffin for you, and a Dr. Pepper for us to share!"

"Thanks," I said sitting down across from him at a two-person booth.

"How was your weekend?" he asked holding my hand across the table.

"It was good, very busy but good. Carly has been dating a guy since Christmas and didn't tell my dad."

"I bet he was really happy about that," Hunter joked.

"Did things get any better with your parents?" I asked taking the conversation on a deeper level.

He gave an exasperated laugh, "No, not really. I'm so done with that whole situation." I knew by the expression on his face that I needed to change the subject.

"Carter wants you to come over one night while he's home so we can all hang out. I'll make him promise not to ask you any questions," with that I gave him a smile.

"I don't really know him so that would be nice," he gently squeezed my hand he was still holding onto across the table. "I'm sorry I haven't called much this week. I guess I haven't been a very good boyfriend lately."

His words made my heart soar. It was just what I needed to hear from him.

"Just because things are hard at home doesn't give me an excuse to ignore you, so I'm sorry."

"It's perfectly okay."

He kissed my hand and minutes later we got back in our cars and made the ten minute drive to school. Driving down the road I passed several gas stations and two banks. The only exciting things we had in town were a Peebles, a Mexican restaurant and a frozen yogurt shop. I'd say the highlight was the old fashioned drug store still on main street that served fresh orangeades and Coke-a-Cola.

"Audrey, Brooklyn, Kara!" I shouted when my three closest friends came into sight in the hallway at school. Audrey and I had been friends since first grade when we moved from Tennessee to right outside of Rockingham,

North Carolina where we had lived since. From day one we were inseparable. I met Brooklyn in fifth grade. Neither of us were blessed in the area of sports so at PE we were always the last ones standing when they chose teams for dodge ball. It was while we waited to see who would be the last one chosen we became good friends. Kara had just moved to Rockingham in ninth grade and from the start she fit in with us perfectly.

"Hey girl!" they shouted back in unison.

"How was your weekend?" I asked walking up to them.

"All right, nothing exciting." Audrey answered. Usually she had some crazy story about her three younger sisters and the mishaps that take place with four girls in the house.

"Yeah, me neither. What about you?" Brooklyn asked.

"Well, Carter came home from Uganda, and at lunch yesterday we found out that Carly had a secret boyfriend she didn't tell my dad about." We all laughed as the bell rang and we separated to go to our classes.

"Hey Chrissy! You're going to New York, right?" one of my friends asked in passing.

"I sure am!" I replied. Brief conversations took place between friends here and there, and I tried to avoid a conversation with my ex-boyfriend when he walked by. Sure, we only dated for three months in ninth grade but he was a very dramatic person and didn't care much for me since I had broken up with him.

"Today we will be discussing..." I couldn't have been more bored. I'm pretty sure that history teacher sucked the life out of each and every student in his class. When that class was over, I headed to something even worse than history. Math.

"Good morning students. On Friday I told everyone there would be a quiz today, so I hope that you studied!" *Stink. Didn't study at all.* I thought. With Carter coming home, and Carly having a secret boyfriend, how could someone remember to study for a geometry quiz? I didn't have to guess at all of the problems, just some, maybe half, just the topics we had covered recently. In all reality one bad grade wasn't going to hurt by B+ average.

"Pencils down." The teacher came around the room and collected our tests, then explained a lesson to us and gave us our homework assignments. When we were dismissed, everyone bolted out of the classroom, and to their next class. Spring fever was setting in big time and everybody, including the teachers were ready for summer.

Just one more class and then lunch, I thought, *Art class and chorus won't be so bad after lunch but all the homework when I get home? Not very much fun.* Finally lunch came and Audrey, Brooklyn, Kara, Hunter, two of his friends, and I all gathered around one of the round tables in the cafeteria.

"How did you do on that math quiz?" Hunter asked me.

"Considering I totally forgot about it, I probably failed." This would have been the time where he should have said, "No, baby, you're too smart to fail." But all I got was, "I'm sorry." *What happened to this whole "being a better boyfriend" speech? That was totally a moment where he could have been a better boyfriend.* He was a math whiz and I was extremely jealous of his ability to do every problem in his head, not study, and still make A's on every test.

Although that irritated me, I mentioned New York, "So, Hunter, we will have dated for two years this summer!"

"We will, won't we? Crazy how time flies." He said taking another bite of his sandwich. Hoping he would mention celebrating our two year anniversary I waited a few seconds before saying, "I think we'll be in New York on our anniversary!"

"Well we will have to do something special while we're there!"

Close enough.

Two classes and a bunch of homework assignments later, I saw Audrey and Brooklyn by their elaborately decorated lockers and shouted to them, "Girls, you ready to go?"

"Yep, I'm coming," Audrey shouted.

"Be right there, let me grab my stuff out of my locker." Brooklyn said over her shoulder. Audrey and Brooklyn were coming over to my house for the afternoon to do homework, and I was driving since neither of them had cars. We never really did our homework when we would hang out, that was mainly an excuse for us to have some girl time. Turning up the radio, we all drove down the road belting out a classic Taylor Swift. I'm sure those driving by had a good laugh. The windows were rolled down letting in the warm spring breeze that was blowing our hair all over the place. When we got back to my house, we grabbed some Oreos and milk from the kitchen and ran upstairs to my room. The time got away from us as we ate our snack and laughed over stories from our various classes throughout the day.

"So, when we're in New York this summer, we need to go to all of those ridiculously expensive stores," Audrey said.

I laughed and replied, "You know none of us can afford any of that stuff."

"It would still be fun just to say we've been there!" Audrey noted.

"That's true. Did they decide which broadway play we're going to see?" Brooklyn asked.

"I think it's between Lion King, Annie and Wicked," I said.

"I vote Wicked, I've heard it's spectacular and it's one of my favorites, but it is Broadway, so I'm sure it's all crazy good," Audrey chimed in as her cell phone dinged.

"Who's that?" I asked.

"My mom, she's here. I guess I've got to go. See you guys tomorrow!" She yelled as she made her way down the stairs and out the front door. After Brooklyn left, I ran downstairs to the kitchen. Something was being cooked, and honestly, it didn't smell very good.

"Mom, what's for dinner?" I asked walking in the kitchen expecting Mom to be standing at the stove cooking up something for supper.

"I don't know what Mom's fixing since she's not home, but I'm making dessert," Carter replied.

"Since when do you cook?" I asked surprised.

"Since I went to Uganda. Rob and Amber taught me how to make a lot of African dishes."

"Well, I'm impressed!"

"Thanks. How was school today?"

"All right I guess, but I totally forgot about the math quiz we had, so I probably failed that. Besides that, it was fine. My history teacher has to be the most boring teacher in the whole school."

"What's his name? I remember my history teacher was really boring, too."

"Mr. Minler."

"I believe that was him!"

"Mom's home!" I yelled when I heard the back door creak open. My mom works as a receptionist at the nearby hospital and Dad is the vice-president of a family owned company.

"Carter, you cook?" Mom asked shocked as she walked in.

43

"I asked the same thing!" we both laughed as he continued to pour more ingredients and stir his concoction, which looked interesting to say the least.

"What's for dinner?" Dad asked as he walked in the door and up the steps to change out of his suit and tie he was wearing.

"I had Carter put the buffalo chicken enchiladas in the oven a while ago, but Carter is making dessert!" Mom shouted from their room.

"Just five more minutes, and then they will be done."

"What is it?" I asked.

"Mandazi; they are made from flour, milk, sugar, baking powder and salt, you mix it and then deep fry it! They are so good."

"Sounds good!" We all sat down at the kitchen table and then Dad's phone rang.

"It's your sister, I better take this," he said getting up and we waited for him before we started eating.

"Hey Carly. How are you? I'm good. Yes. Okay, that should be fine, but you know my rule- no hanging out by yourselves in your room, and we spent time together. Good. All right. Love you too, bye." We could just hear his part of the conversation. I had a good idea of what they were talking about and as they spoke I could feel the tenseness in the room rising by the moment.

Dad sat back down at the table and I grabbed my fork to begin taking my first bite of enchilada. Before putting it in my mouth I noticed Carter looking at us all waiting to pray.

"Can I?" he began.

"Oh, of course," Mom's cheeks turned pink.

"Heavenly Father, we thank you for this beautiful day you have so graciously given us. I am so thankful for this time together with my family. I ask You to continue to shape us according to Your will and Your plan for us. Guide us in Your grace and love. We love you, Lord. Bless this food to the nourishment of our bodies. It's in Your Name we pray, amen."

After a few seconds passed, Mom asked impatiently, "Well, what did she say?"

"She said that she gets out of school on Friday and that she will be going with Nathan Saturday morning to meet his parents. Then they will be driving back to our house Saturday night. She wanted to know if it was okay if he stayed the night here on Saturday."

"What did you say?" I asked.

"I told her that would be fine, but she had to remember that we all hang out together and they're not allowed to be alone in her room."

"Ok. Well at least we get to meet him," Mom said not quite content with all of this secret boyfriend thing. This coming weekend was going to be quite interesting for the whole family.

Chapter 4

As I woke up Saturday morning I could smell bacon from downstairs and only hoped for Mom's homemade chocolate chip pancakes. I rolled over in bed and glanced at my phone. The time read 9:45. Throwing my blankets off of me I stood up and rubbed my eyes before putting my glasses on. After sliding a comfy sweatshirt over my head, I walked downstairs and found Mom in the kitchen drinking coffee.

"I could have sworn I smelled bacon." I looked at her with questioning eyes when I didn't see any food on the counters.

"It's all in the oven, I kept it warm for you."

Walking to the fridge, I pulled out the container of orange juice and poured myself a glass. The bacon and chocolate chip pancakes were warm, just as Mom had promised.

Moments later Carter came through the back door, drenched in sweat.

"How was your run?" Mom asked, taking another sip of coffee.

"Great! I ran almost three miles." He downed almost an entire bottle of water. Within seconds he was walking up to me and engulfed me in a hug before I could do anything about it.

"Ew!" I squirmed out of his arms, "You're gross."

"You know you love me!" He backed up and started to run upstairs. I sat down at the bar and began to dig into my breakfast.

"I do!" I said through a mouth full of pancakes.

Carter hadn't gotten half way up the stairs when he shouted, "What time is Carly coming home?"

"I completely forgot about that!" I turned to Mom and waited for her answer.

"They'll get here just in time for dinner," she walked to the kitchen and put her coffee cup in the sink." I need you two to go get some stuff for dinner."

"Okay," Carter and I responded in unison. I hurried to finish my breakfast and went to shower before we headed to the store to get whatever Mom needed for this grand dinner occasion.

At five o'clock that night we heard a car pull into the driveway. I glanced out the living room window from where I was sitting and saw Nathan open Carly's door. Carter was sitting beside me and I looked to him shrugging my shoulders. We shared a quiet laugh. Neither of us quite knew what to think about him.

"Mom, Dad!" She said as we all walked out on to the front porch to greet them.

"This is Nathan," she said holding hands with him and walking up the path to the front door.

"It's very nice to meet you all. Carly has told me so much about you!" he said shaking hands with Mom and Dad who had gone out to her car to greet them.

"Nice to meet you too, Nathan," Dad said insincerely. I stood on the porch waiting for them to come inside.

"Nathan, would you help me get my stuff out of the car?" my sister asked.

"Of course!" he rushed to her side and helped her carry in all of her stuff.

"Carly, where do you want this?" He asked as he carried a suitcase inside the house, stopping to shake Carter's hand.

"Nice to meet you, man," Carter said with a smile, assuring him that he was welcome after Dad's cold greeting.

"You too," Nathan gave a slight smile before turning to Carly who was already half way up the stairs.

"I'll show you where my bedroom is," she responded as she made her way in the house and up the stairs to her bedroom on the left.

"Can you put it in here?" She asked pointing to her lime-green painted bedroom.

"Wow! Check out this color," he joked. I could hear their exchange from my bedroom across the hall.

"Hey!" She playfully slapped his arm, "The last time we painted in here was when I was fourteen." It's true. That same lime-green color had been on the walls for seven years. Aside from that, her double bed was in the middle of the room neatly made with the pillows perfectly arranged. Dust covered the picture frames she hadn't taken with her to school and all the boxes brought in were full of things to hang back up on the walls while she was home for the summer.

"Carly, Nathan, Chrissy, dinner is ready," Dad shouted from downstairs.

"We're coming," Carly replied and I could hear Nathan kiss her on the cheek. I ran down the stairs right before they did.

"Nathan?" Dad inquired once we were all seated. *Oh gosh,* I thought, not knowing what he would ask." Would you mind saying the blessing?"

"Not at all," he bowed his head and began, "Lord, thank you for this time together tonight, help us to continue to bring glory to you as we go through the next couple of days, and bless this food you have so graciously given us, amen."

Everyone began eating, and an awkward silence ensued. No one quite knew what to say.

"So, Nathan, what do you want to do once you graduate?" my dad questioned, breaking the silence.

"Well, I plan on continuing my education after undergrad. My major now is English and Literature and I hope to complete my Master of Arts in Education. From there I would love to teach at a college level," he responded.

My dad just nodded, I could tell he was trying to figure this guy out.

"I've shared this with Carly but in high school I hated all things reading and writing. I wasn't sure what I wanted to major in when I first came to Gardner-Webb. We were all required to take at least two English courses and I was dreading it. The first day of class I sat down at my desk and when the teacher started talking, my dislike for English completely faded. Mr. Tucker was his name, he was, by far, the best teacher I've ever had. From that day on I have felt the Lord's calling to teach that very subject. I definitely didn't see it coming but I know it's what He wants me to do," Nathan continued.

"That's awesome," Mom responded.

"Thank you," he replied.

We talked about church and family and other stuff that I couldn't have cared less about. I had figured out that Nathan's Dad was a pastor, he was a couple months older than Carly, and he had a Bible study with other guys on campus once a week. After we all finished eating, the conversation proceeded, but I grabbed some dishes and headed to the sink. Nathan gathered the remaining plates and suddenly appeared behind me.

"So, Carly's told me a lot about you," Nathan said.

Well she sure hasn't told us a whole lot about you, I thought, but decided that *probably* wouldn't be the best thing to say.

"You're a junior, right?" He asked, trying to carry on simple, yet really awkward conversation, as we walked back to the table.

"Yep."

"Are you looking at colleges yet?"

"Not much, I've looked at a few, but nothing seriously."

"Well Gardner-Webb is pretty great. You should consider it."

I nodded as we sat back down at the table, glad that conversation was over. I never know what to say in situations like that.

"Can I come in?" I asked knocking on Carly's partially open door later that night. When I peeked in the door I saw she and Nathan sitting on her bed talking. *If only Dad knew about this,* I thought. Sure, they were only talking but he still wouldn't have been happy.

When she didn't respond I walked on in, disrupting whatever was going on.

"Oh hey! Come on in," she sat patting the spot beside her on the bed, "You wanna play a game of cards?"

"Sure, what game?"

"Hyjack, I'll totally beat you!" Nathan blurted out as a joke.

"How do you play? By the way, I will win after I get the hang of it." I jumped up on her double bed and sat beside her and Nathan as she explained the game to me. During the game I also learned that Nathan was the opposite of Carly when it came to games, he was very, very competitive.

"It's almost twelve, I'm gonna head downstairs, all right?" Nathan said, jumping off the bed and leaning down to kiss Carly on the cheek.

"I'll walk you down," she followed him out the door after turning to me and saying, "I'll be right back!"

I nodded at her. Before they had made it out of earshot they were already in conversation. Nathan's voice came first.

"I'm sorry I've been so nervous."

"It's okay, I understand."

"I really like your sister," he added just as they stepped far enough away so that I couldn't hear them. As I sat in the silence of her room, I could only think about how much I had missed our time together. Normally when she came home the first thing we did was go out for ice cream and spend hours laughing and talking together. But with Nathan around that hadn't been possible.

"Okay, finally," Carly said walking back in her room five minutes later.

I just laughed as we slipped under the blankets together. We used to have sister sleepovers all the time. We would stay up late sharing about secret crushes and school and how Mom and Dad were constantly getting on our nerves. I had a feeling this would be one of those nights.

"I like him, I do," I assured her once we had settled in.

"I'm glad, he was so nervous," she gave a compassionate smile.

"It wasn't too evident."

"Good. So how are you and Hunter?" She asked looking right into my eyes. *Here comes conversation number two I've been dreading. You can do this, Chrissy!*

"Pretty good, his parents have been fighting a lot, so it's been hard on him."

"Has he been going to church?"

"I knew you were going to ask this."

"So why didn't you come up with a good answer?" She asked laughing.

"Let's just put it this way, he's gone about as much as we have lately."

"And how much is that?"

"Not a whole lot," I said hesitantly.

"You know you need to be going every week, Chrissy." Her eyes told me she had never been more serious.

"I know." Another pang of guilt hit my chest.

"Why haven't you guys been going?"

"I don't know, when Carter left we slowly stopped going, he was the one who always wanted to go anyway. With you gone too I just didn't have a whole lot of encouragement. Yes, Mom and Dad wanted to go but it wasn't their first priority."

"But you used to love church."

"I know, I guess it's not as fun as it used to be. When I was in middle school conversations were still fun and lighthearted. Now they're full of pressure and convictions and it's," I paused, realizing what I was about to say didn't feel right for one reason or another, "uncomfortable."

"First of all, church isn't just about having fun at your age. It's about growing in your faith and fellowshipping with other believers who will encourage you in your walk with Christ."

"I know. You've told me that a million times." She had told me that statement multiple times over the past few years and it resonated in my brain.

"And I'll tell you a million more."

Awkward silence.

"So, what do you really think of him?" She asked perking up a little.

"Nathan?"

"Yes, who else would I be talking about!"

"He's better than all the other guys you've dated, and that's only after a couple of hours!"

"Well that's for sure," her cheeks began to turn pink.

"He's funny, loves the Lord from what I can see, and is respectful to us all, but..."

"But what?" Her gorgeous blue eyes widened.

"Does he love you?"

"Of course, why would you wonder that?" She relaxed a bit.

"I guess I just wanted to hear it from you."

54

"He's a really good guy and different than the other guys I've dated. I really do love him, and he loves me." I tried to get a glimpse of how she felt about Nathan. *This, I told myself, This is love. She's completely smitten with him.* Everything about that moment made me suddenly second guess what I had with Hunter. *Hunter is a great guy!* I assured myself.

"Is he a keeper?" I looked her in the eyes. *She really adores him,* I couldn't help but thinking again.

"I think he is," she said smiling at me and I knew that this really was different, even if she had kept it from Dad.

Chapter 5

"Just one more week of school, and then I get you all
to myself," my brother said Monday morning walking in
the door from his daily run. As I drove to school, I
thought about our weekend. Nathan had left Sunday
night after a long day of church, lunch, and a competitive
family game of Monopoly. I would say that our weekend
with the secret boyfriend had gone pretty well, and that
everyone, including Mom and Dad liked him. Sunday
night after Nathan had left I called Hunter to check up on
him and see how things were at home.

"Hunter?"

"Hey Chrissy, I texted you a couple times, why didn't
you call?" He seemed upset.

"Sorry, Carly came home with her boyfriend this
weekend. How have you been?"

"I'm all right. My parents are getting a divorce, it's
final. That's why I wanted to call you."

"Oh Hunter, I'm so sorry." I tried to let compassion ring through in my voice, only hoping he could hear it over the phone.

"I think my dad's moving out but I'm not sure where he's going." His frustration was evident, just like every other time we had talked within the past couple of weeks.

"I wish none of this had ever happened, it's been so hard on you."

"Yeah, me neither, but you've been right there beside me the whole time, so thanks."

"You're welcome, that's what I'm here for. I miss you, Hunter," I paused hoping for a tender response.

"I miss you, too." *Nothing.* I thought. *Well, he has been through a lot lately. Give him a break.*

"How 'bout we grab some dinner tomorrow night? Maybe it would help get your mind off of things. My brother wanted us to come with him and some of his friends from college."

"That would be awesome. See you at school."

"See you then." Without another word we both hung up. Minutes later I was standing in front of the mirror taking off my makeup when it hit me: he didn't tell me he loved me. And I didn't tell him, either. But for some reason, that fact didn't hurt me like I thought it would. I just knew that wasn't a good sign.

He was clearly stressed out. I knew his parent's divorce was weighing on him, but he just wasn't the Hunter I knew. He wasn't my fun, energetic boyfriend. And I missed that.

"Hey," I said walking up to him at school the next day. I wrapped my arms around him and I could smell my favorite cologne on his plaid Hollister shirt.

"How are you?" I asked looking in his deep brown eyes, the ones I had loved since the beginning. He was a totally different person than he had been over the phone the night before.

"Better, I think it helped getting out of the house." He smiled at me and we walked hand in hand to my locker.

"Good, it makes me sad seeing you like that. I know this has to be so stressful."

"It's all so overwhelming. It's a lot to deal with."

"Yeah," I tried to get a glimpse of what he was feeling, "So do you want to come to church with me this Sunday?" *Did I really just ask him that? He's never liked church!*

"I don't know."

"Oh, well, just think about it, okay? I've gone the past two weeks."

"I will." He squeezed my hand he was still holding. To get his mind off of things, we talked about my weekend with Nathan and Carly. But by the time Audrey, Brooklyn, and Kara came up he was easily distracted due to their constant conversations. Soon we headed into class, and I counted down the minutes until I got to get in my car, head home, eat oreos, and talk to my big brother and sister.

After 420 minutes of Mr. Minler's history lectures, chemistry, math, and listening Kara to talk about her Mom's twenty cats, I got in my bug, popped in another Taylor Swift CD and drove home.

"Hey, you're home! How was school?" Carly asked as I passed her room on my way to my room.

"It was school, all right. Who did you have for history?" I asked walking into her room.

"Some guy. He was really boring."

"Mr. Minler?"

"Yeah, why?"

"I have him too."

"Oh, sorry." I leaned over her shoulder, as she sat at her desk, looking at Facebook.

"Are you going with me, Hunter, Carter, and Stephen to dinner?"

"I don't know. Wait, who's Stephen? I thought you were dating Hunter?" She asked jokingly.

I rolled my eyes at her, "One of the guys Carter went to school with."

"Oh, I might."

"Mom and Dad are going on a date."

"Then, yes, I will be going with you. Wait, did you say Hunter is coming?"

"Yes, why?"

"It just surprised me. Have you tried inviting him to go to church with you yet?"

"I did this morning, actually."

"And he said?"

"He pretty much said no." I walked out, ending that conversation, and headed to my room. I had hoped for a light-hearted conversation after a long day at school but I could feel that was not where she was headed. I was desperate to get my mind off of the conversations pulling at my heart between both of my older siblings. My Pinterest feed was full of summer clothes ideas that only made me wish for days at the pool even more.

My phone vibrated in my lap interrupting my daydreaming. It was a text from Carter." Mom needs me to run some errands while I am out. Be back in less than an hour."

We planned on meeting everyone at Don Juan's, our favorite mexican restaurant in town, around six. When the clock hit four thirty, I figured I should get some homework done before dinner.

I got a text from Hunter an hour later on our way to the restaurant, "I'm not going to be able to make it tonight. Sticky situation at home, Mom said I had to be here." *He's never cancelled on a date before. That's really weird*, I thought.

"Hey, Carter, Hunter isn't going to be able to make it," I said disappointedly. We hadn't been to dinner in forever, and the only time we had seen each other was at school. I responded to his text, "We will miss you. Need to hang out soon. Okay?"

"Why can't he come?" Carly asked.

I reopened the text and read it to her.

"Sounds serious," Carter said pulling into the parking lot of our favorite mexican restaurant.

"They're officially getting a divorce, did I not tell you?"

"That was me," Carly said raising her hand.

During dinner Carter shared with Stephen his experiences from Uganda. Even though I had heard all of Carter's stories multiple times, I couldn't help but be drawn to the conversation. Most of this was due to the fact that Stephen was a college graduate with bright blue eyes, perfect hair and just tall enough to satisfy my liking. His laughter filled the room and I felt guilty for being attracted to him when I had a boyfriend. *You've got Hunter,* I said to myself, *and he's a great guy.*

Once we got home, I picked back up with my homework, texted some friends for a while, and went to bed with a glorious thought in my mind. Only four more days of school, which meant only 1,680 more minutes of Mr. Minler, chemistry and Kara's cat conversations for the rest of the semester.

Chapter 6

Starting Tuesday final exams began and by the end of the week my brain was completely fried. Despite my lack of love and devotion for exams, I was thankful we were spared the tedious monologues of Mr. Minler. That afternoon I headed home and with no homework to do - only a beautiful, warm, carefree summer to look forward to.

Carly, Carter and I watched *Hairspray* together singing all of the songs and even throwing in a few dances here and there. The rest of the day was rather uneventful. We had dinner and played Wii for a while, and then I headed up to my room and grabbed my phone, dialing Hunter's number.

He didn't answer so I just left a message, "Hey, Hunter, it's me, Chrissy. I was just calling to check on you and see if you wanted to do dinner sometime. Hope you had a good day. Call me back soon, love you. Bye." *What's up with him? Canceling on a date, not answering my calls?* I was starting to worry. And honestly, I just wanted my boyfriend back. The same boyfriend who had just told me weeks earlier he was going to try to do better.

"Hey Chrissy," Carter knocked and came into my room.

"What's up?" He asked, sitting down at the foot of my bed.

"Nothing much."

"Have you talked to Hunter much lately?" He asked after seeing my phone still open to the missed call.

"Um, no, not really. I mean I talked to him at school today briefly but that's about it."

"Is that like him?"

"Not at all. We normally talk throughout the day, I don't know what's up with him."

I didn't want to say anything else because that whole God conversation could have easily come up.

"Do you want to go and get some and coffee tomorrow?" He asked, breaking the silence.

"I would love to!" With that I relaxed because I knew this would be just like our old, big brother-little sister coffee dates we used to have together.

The next morning I got up at about 9:00 and started fixing my breakfast, relieved that I didn't have school for the next two months.

"Morning, Chrissy," Carter said as he walked into the kitchen. I could tell he had just come back from a run due to the beads of sweat on his forehead and the dampness of his shirt, "Why are you fixing breakfast?"

"Because I'm hungry." *A girl has got to eat*, I thought, giving him a curious look.

"But I thought we were going to breakfast?"

"We are?"

"Yeah, remember yesterday I asked you if you wanted to grab some coffee?" He looked at me, obviously seeing I didn't remember our conversation from the night before.

"I thought you meant later."

"No, I meant for breakfast!"

"Well I am good with that too, let me run upstairs," he stopped me mid-sentence.

"Slow down, you've got about 20 minutes, I still have to get a quick shower and then we'll go."

"Carter, it will take me 20 minutes to get ready," I gave him a slight eye roll.

"Well then, hurry up!" he said as we raced up the stairs. I was in mid-change when my door began to open, "I'm changing!" I shouted.

"Hurry," Carly yelled. *What hurry was she in?*

"What?" I said opening my door, after I had changed.

"What are you and Carter doing?"

"Going to breakfast."

"Can I come?" she asked desperate to have a reason to get out of the house. All of her close friends lived near Gardner-Webb so she had no one to hang out with besides Carter and me.

"Not to be rude, but no."

"What?" she asked raising her voice like I had just insulted the president.

"This is our big-brother, little-sister breakfast date," I replied, rolling my eyes.

"Okay, fine. But I want to take you to breakfast sometime next week then."

"All right, now can I get ready?" I said as she walked away. Once I had pulled my hair up into a cute pony tail, Carter and I headed out the door and hopped in my bug.

"I'll drive," Carter said, as we approached the car.

"What, you don't think I'm a good driver?" I made my way around to the passenger side.

"No, I know you are a good driver, but it's early, and your head is probably still a bit foggy," he said laughing, as he started the car. Once we got to our favorite breakfast spot, he parked and we walked inside.

"Table for two, please," he stated.

"Right this way," the waitress pointed us to a table and we ordered our coffees. As I added the fifth packet of sugar to my cup, I came to the conclusion that maybe I wasn't a coffee drinker quite yet. We talked for a while, enjoying our big brother-little sister time. We talked about Africa and friends, about all of the people he had met there. I discovered there were new stories yet to be told about his time in Uganda. I hoped all morning that the God conversation wouldn't come up because that would ruin all the fun of our morning outing.

"Can I drive? I don't think I'm foggy headed anymore," I asked walking to my car after we had finished eating.

"Alright, did you bring your license?"

"Of course! I always bring it." We got in my car and he used his iPhone to play some Christian music that I had never heard before, but for once, I actually liked it.

"I know you've been avoiding this conversation but I'm worried about you, Chrissy. You don't seem like the same kid I left two years ago." *And it's happening.*

Keeping my eyes on the road ahead of me, I didn't say anything.

"Is there something going on that I don't know about?" *Here we go. I'm gonna have to spill it.*

"No. Well, I don't know. I guess I've just changed."

"There's more to it than that. Please be honest with me. You know you can tell me anything." His tone held an amount of desperation I had never heard from him before.

I took a deep breath and began to speak, "I guess it just started when you left..."

My breath was taken away when Carter suddenly shouted, "Chrissy, watch out!" as he threw himself across me; guarding my body with his own. All I could see was another car coming quickly towards mine.

~~~~~~~~

My head started to spin as I tried to gain control of the car. It was useless. We spun in circles and suddenly everything went black and a sharp pain ran through my head. The next thing I heard were sirens and unfamiliar voices shouting words I couldn't comprehend.

Where am I? What's going on?

"Chrissy, can you hear me?" someone asked.

I just nodded as I slowly opened my eyes. My head pounded.

"Does anything hurt?" the same voice questioned.

"Just my head," was all I could respond without feeling dizzy.

"You were unconscious for a few minutes but you will be able to think clearly in just a little while." I took in my surroundings. Frantically searching the ambulance I could not find Carter. Panic filled my chest and I reminded myself to keep breathing.

"Where's my brother? Is he okay?" I asked nervously. Things started to make sense. It was all coming back to me. The instantaneous shattering of my car, Carter leaning over to guard my body, excruciating pain striking my forehead as it hit the steering wheel and I lost control of the vehicle.

"He's hurt, but he will be okay. We think he broke his leg, maybe his foot, but we aren't sure. We are on our way to the hospital." My face felt hot and wet. I reached my hand up to feel my cheek. It came away wet but not with the blood as I feared it would, only

67

with the tears I was unconsciously crying. As they continued streaming down my face my thoughts began to clarify and I wondered, *why did this have to happen?*

"All right, we're here," one of the paramedics announced. Pulling up, they unloaded the stretcher I was laying on from the ambulance and everyone else piled out. Mom ran out of the hospital and came immediately to where they were unloading Carter and I from our ambulances. I was allowed to stand with the help of a paramedic. I walked over to her, hugging her so tightly that she probably couldn't breathe. She kissed my head over and over again, as my tears poured onto her shirt.

"Thank God you are okay."

"Mom, it's all my fault that Carter got hurt," from out of nowhere this sickening feeling of guilt was piling up inside of me.

"No it's not. That car hit you, you didn't hit the car." With her arm over my shoulder we walked into the hospital and one of the paramedics told us they had wheeled Carter into the x-ray room.

"She was unconscious for a little while, so we are going to need to do some x-rays just to make sure everything is okay," one of the paramedics told us. We both nodded; they put me in a wheelchair and took me on back. Mom was waiting right outside the door for me and she held me tightly, guiding me to the waiting room.

They had said nothing was wrong. That I was fine. They didn't know how I felt inside, how broken I really felt. Tears silently fell down my cheeks. *How bad was Carter? Was he okay?* I thought.

"Chrissy?" my mom said loudly, she had been talking to me." Are you thirsty, do you want something to drink?" she asked and I finally snapped back into reality.

"Um," my head pounded as I tried to think, "Just some water and some ibuprofen would be great, too." She turned and whispered something to a nurse standing nearby. I closed my eyes and Mom held me close as the tears started to run more quickly down my face. A paramedic and police officer came up to us.

"Ma'am," one of them said, "Could you describe what happened to you?"

"Sure," it was all still so fresh in my mind, I could see the scene replaying itself." We had breakfast and were driving home. I had the right of way but the other car ran a stop sign. He rammed into the side of my car spinning us in circles. At some point I blacked out, so I don't know what happened after that."

"It's a miracle your daughter wasn't seriously hurt, the same with your son," the officer said, jotting something down on the clipboard he was holding.

"God was protecting them the whole time," my mom said leaning over and kissing me on the forehead as they walked away. I heard the elevator ding just seconds later. The door opened and I saw Carly's wavy brown hair first, then Dad's face creased with worry. Carly walked quickly over to me and I stood and hugged her with everything in me, as her tears dropped onto my shoulder.

I could hear her breathing deeply, "I'm so glad you're okay," she whispered. Moments later one of the doctors came to find us, clipboard in hand, "Are you all Carter's family?"

"Yes, sir," Mom answered.

"Come on back," he said, leading us to the ER.

"Now, when Carter leaned over in the car, it caused his legs and feet to get stuck under the dash, this caused multiple fractures in his right leg and right foot. His foot is the worst with a comminuted fracture that will need reconstructive surgery as soon as possible," he informed us before we walked in.

"Will he be okay?" At this point Dad's arm was wrapped around my side assuring me that everything really was going to be okay.

"Yes, he will be fine. It's a miracle he wasn't hurt any more than he was. We need to do the surgery either later today or early in the morning, depending on the last time he ate. I will let you all know when they find a time slot. I've got to go check on my other patients. The nurses will be here in about thirty minutes and transfer him to a regular room," He said and then walked away as if Carter was just another patient to check off his list.

The next thing I remember seeing was not my strong big brother who always held me when I cried and took me to breakfast to catch up. I saw a crushed Carter lying on the hospital bed dressed in a hospital gown, with his leg propped up off the bed. He looked nearly defeated. I ran up to his bed, sat down and buried my head gently in his shoulder. Again tears fell down my cheeks as I sat with my arms hugging him. He wrapped his arms around my small body and comforted me as I cried. No words were needed. After about five minutes of silence, I knew it was time to stop crying and get it together. As I sat up I noticed the tears falling down Carter's cheeks, too.

"I'm so glad you are okay," he said to me, trying to hold it together.

"But you aren't." I wiped my hand under my eyes.

"I will be. It's just my leg."

"And your foot."

"Yeah, but at least it's not any worse. The nurse gave me some pain medication, and it is slowly starting to work."

"Good, I got here as fast as I could once your Mom called me," Dad said. For a minute I had forgotten that the rest of the family was even in the room.

"He had to pick me up first because I don't have a car," Carly said, "By the way, Carter, nice dress!" She was always the one to make everybody smile.

"Thanks," he said and we all half-heartedly laughed. The nurses soon came and took him to a room. Carly and Dad headed to get some lunch for everybody from the cafeteria while Mom and I stayed in the room with Carter. The hospital room was large compared to others with a chair in one corner and a couch that would also serve as a bed on the other wall. There was a TV and counter with a sink that also had the computer to the left of it but nothing could take away from the sterile smell. I moved from Carter's bedside and sat beside Mom on the couch, "It's all my fault."

"No it's not. I already told you, that car hit you."

"I know the car hit us."

"Then what's your fault?" With the greatest care she ran her hands through my hair.

"Carter getting hurt. He was leaning over to protect me." I tilted my head and looked her in the eyes.

"Honey, a protective big brother's first instinct is to keep his sister from danger and that's what he did. He knows it's his job. The doctor also said that him leaning over saved him from being hurt even worse."

"Carter always protects me, and when it mattered most I did nothing to protect him, that's what matters," I said burying my head in her shoulder and she wrapped her arms around me, having nothing left to say.

Chapter 7

"Thanks," I said grabbing a piece of pizza from Dad's hand. He sat our drinks down on the table beside the couch.

"You're welcome." He took a quick glance at Carter before sitting down beside Mom." How long has he been asleep?"

"Ever since ya'll left. I think it's because Carly wouldn't quit talking," I joked.

Thirty minutes later we heard a knock at the door and our pastor walked in.

"How is he?" he whispered.

"He's hanging in there," my dad told him as he stood up to shake his hand.

"What happened?"

"Chrissy and Carter went to breakfast and they were on the way back when a car hit the passenger side of Chrissy's car. It broke his right leg and his right foot."

"Oh my goodness. It's a miracle that Chrissy didn't get hurt."

"Yes, it is. He's going to have surgery to reconstruct his foot," Dad continued.

"Jim, what are you doing here?" Carter inquired groggily.

"I came to see you, how are you?"

"I've been better," Carter said, "but I'll be all right. Thanks for coming." Every time he spoke my heart was crushed.

"You're very welcome. Candice and the kids sent some cards," he said giving Carter a handful of cards.

He smiled, "Tell them I said thanks."

"I will. Do you guys need anything? I see you've already had lunch," he said, seeing our leftover cups." Can we get you some dinner? Oh, sorry to mention food, Carter. You probably can't eat, can you?"

Carter shook his head.

"I think we're good for now, but thank you," Mom replied.

"I know you're probably tired, Carter," he said looking over at him, "But can I pray with you all before I leave?"

"Absolutely," Dad didn't hesitate.

Everyone bowed their heads, eyes closed.

"Our gracious Heavenly Father, we come to you this afternoon and I just want to thank you for protecting Chrissy and Carter. Though Carter is hurt, you kept them safe and we are so thankful. I ask that you comfort Carter and bring him healing through this time of restoration. I know you will be with this family every step of these months ahead and I ask that you would make yourself so real to them that they could feel you. Thank you for promising healing in every area of our lives. We love you, Lord. Amen."

Mom's eyes were brimming with tears as she stood.

"If you need anything, please call me."

"We will, thank you," Mom said, hugging him before he left.

I heard my phone buzz in my pocket before the door had clicked shut. I hoped it was one of two people: Audrey or Hunter.

OH MY GOSH. I saw your Mom's Facebook post! ARE YOU OKAY???

Audrey's text lifted my spirits, if only for a moment, as I quickly typed, *Yes, I'm fine. Carter's hurt pretty badly but we both made it out okay. It was terrifying.*

Seconds later her response showed up on my screen.

I'm so glad. I was SO worried. Can I do anything?? Bring you some Sour Patch Kids?

I think we're set right now, but I'll definitely let you know. Thank you for checking in on us. I'm hurt... just not physically.

Understandable. Love you, girl. Thinking about you guys.

Thanks. Love you, too. Oh, and please let Hunter know I'm okay. I don't want him to be worried.

Will do!

I locked my phone and slid it in my pocket, desperate for the doctor to come in. I needed to know what was next, needed to know what the next few days would look like.

The hours seemed to crawl by, each minute taking longer than the one before. By three o'clock Carter's doctor finally made it in.

"Good afternoon," he said. *It's not really a good afternoon*, I thought." Well, I've talked to the nurses and orthopedic surgeons and we can do the surgery first thing in the morning. It could take anywhere from two to six hours, things go differently depending on the patient each time we get in the OR. The nurses will move him to surgery prep at six in the morning. I know it's early but we need to get him in before the scheduled surgeries."

Dad breathed in deeply, "Okay, thank you." Everyone just fell silent. No one knew quite what to say. I just stared off in the distance, willing myself not to begin crying again.

Dad broke the silence, "It's almost time for dinner. Why don't you girls head home, have something to eat and get some sleep? I'll stay with Carter tonight and you all can join us early in the morning before his surgery. I know you'll want to be here to see him before he goes back."

I nodded and Mom stood to grab her purse, "You sure you'll be okay?"

"Absolutely," he kissed Mom on the cheek.

"I'll bring you some clothes and dinner later, okay, honey?" she said to Dad as she opened the door quietly and we walked out.

We picked up some Zaxby's on our way home so Mom wouldn't have to worry about cooking.

Upon arriving, the house was quiet, too quiet. Our night was slow and uneventful. Mom had taken Dad a change of clothes, some snacks and a few other things he had asked for. The three of us watched a movie together, but few words were said. Standing in the bathroom later that night, scrubbing away the stress of the day, I could see the reflection of Carter's room in the mirror. His bible lay open on his bed. Rubbing my eyes, I put my glasses on, changed into sweatpants and a t-shirt, and crawled into my unmade bed. My mind rewound back to that morning, rushing excitedly to get ready for breakfast, pulling up my hair quickly not wanting to keep Carter waiting for me. My heart was so happy that morning. My thoughts were interrupted as my phone rang. I reached for it on my nightstand.

"Hello?" I said groggily, slipping on my glasses again.

"Hey, it's Hunter." He sounded sleepy himself, a bit worried.

I took a deep breath, so glad to be talking to him. Suddenly I couldn't help but start crying.

"Long day?" He said tenderly after a moment.

"Yeah."

"You okay?" His voice was caring and kind, exceedingly more so than the past weeks.

"No, not really." I took a deep breath.

"I saw your mom's Facebook status, what exactly happened?"

"Long story short, a car ran a stop sign, hit us and now Carter is having surgery at six in the morning. It's all my fault."

"No it's not," he assured me." Wait? What surgery?"

"They're having to reconstruct his foot."

"Wow."

"Yeah," I responded, too tired to say more.

"I'm sorry I didn't call earlier."

"It's okay. We just got back from the hospital a couple hours ago."

"You're physically okay, right?"

"Yeah, I'm fine."

"I'm so glad. I was worried sick after I saw your mom's post about Carter." It made me happy to know that he cared, to know that he was worried about me.

"Wanna grab some lunch tomorrow? Maybe it would help to get your mind off of things," he asked.

"I think it'll be okay to leave Carter for a little while."

"What time should I come pick you up?"

"They're not quite sure how long the surgery will last, so I'll text you when he's in post-op."

"Perfect," he paused and then added, "Hey, I love you," he added and I grinned. *There's my Hunter.*

"I love you too, goodnight."

"Goodnight." We both hung up and I crawled back into my bed, anxious for the rest I knew wouldn't come easily.

"Chrissy, baby, you need to get up," Mom whispered coming in my room the next morning." I know it's early but we need to see Carter before he goes back for surgery."

I opened my eyes just enough to see out the window: it was still pitch black. My phone screen read 5:00 am.

"If you want to shower, you need to do it now. We need to leave in the next forty minutes." She moved to the side of my bed and I sat up. Sleep came in waves, but mostly I had tossed and turned all night.

"Did you sleep at all?" She played with my hair and I almost fell back asleep.

I simply shook my head in response.

"Me either."

"You okay this morning?" she asked after waiting a minute or two.

"No, not really. I still feel completely guilty for everything that happened."

"You don't have to feel that way, but I know it's hard not to. All of this is going to be hard, but we'll make it through. It'll get easier, you'll see." Her voice cracked as she continued to play with my hair.

I nodded, doubtful that this would ever get easier.

I got up and picked out some clothes for the day, jeans and a t-shirt, something comfortable enough to wear at the hospital all day. Seeing me go to the bathroom to shower, Mom left to go fix her hair and remind Carly to get up.

We left the house just in time to get to the hospital before they took Carter back to surgery prep.

"Good morning," Dad said, greeting Mom at the door with a kiss on her cheek.

"How are you feeling?" Mom asked Carter.

"I'm okay, didn't sleep much last night. I'm really hungry since I haven't eaten in hours. I mean, that feast of rainbow jello and ice chips last night at ten was so filling." He brought us all laughter; something I was so thankful for. I walked over to his bed and gave him a hug. The nurses were in within the next fifteen minutes and my anxiety was growing by the minute. They gave him a series of medicines through his IV and checked his blood pressure before taking him down to surgery prep.

"Can I come with him?" Dad asked.

"Of course," one of the nurses answered, "And the rest of you can come see him in a few minutes before his anesthesia kicks in."

"Thank you," Carly replied. We followed them back and stood anxiously outside the swinging doors, waiting until we could go back. Dad came to get us a few minutes later and took us to see Carter. The last twenty-four hours flashed before my eyes. The car spinning in circles, the sound of the other car ramming into mine, and finally, Carter saving my life. That too-familiar guilty feeling resurfaced as we stood around Carter who was becoming loopy due to the anesthesia.

"You okay?" Mom asked Carter.

"As okay as it gets," he said.

Dad wrapped his arm around me as a few solitary tear drops fell down my cheeks.

"Let's pray," Dad said. *You're really going to pray? I couldn't help but thinking. How can you not be angry that this happened? And to Carter of all people. Why not me? God, he's living his life out for you and this is what he gets? I don't understand.*

"Lord," Dad paused, clearing his throat in an attempt to keep his tears at bay. This was one of the few times I had ever seen my dad cry." Keep Carter safe. Guide the doctors and surgeons on how to take care of him properly. Help us to trust you and find comfort in you. Amen."

Just then two nurses and the anesthesiologist came up, "Alright, it's time. Carter, the medicine will start working in just a few minutes. You won't feel a thing."

Mom kissed him on the forehead and they took the lock off of his rolling bed.

"I love you, Carter," I said as they wheeled him off. I couldn't take my eyes off of his bed as they rolled it down the hallway and out of view.

"Love you, too," he said. My vision was blurred as I watched them push him down the hallway and into the operating room. Dad's hand was at my back, "Come on, honey. He's going to be fine."

Everything is going to be okay, I thought to myself as we walked to the waiting room, *like Dad said, he's going to be fine. He has to be fine.*

We sat and waited for what seemed like an eternity. Several people came to visit with us so we wouldn't be by ourselves all morning. Carter had been in surgery for over five hours when to my surprise, Hunter walked into the hospital waiting room.

"I didn't text you!" I said, greeting him.

"I thought you could use the company," he said, hugging me and kissing me on the cheek. Being in his arms had never felt so good.

"Hey, Hunter," Carly said opening her eyes, after resting for a little bit. Mom and Dad looked exhausted. I hoped that they would be able to get some rest while I was gone.

"How long has he been in surgery?" he asked.

"Since a little after six this morning," I responded.

"Will it take much longer?"

"No, they should be done any moment now," Mom responded.

Just then one of the OR staff walked up and said, "You're Carter's family?" We all nodded.

"He's just come out of surgery. Everything went just as planned."

"Great," Dad seemed to be able to breathe more normally.

"He'll probably sleep for about an hour, but you all can come on back to post-op."

With my hand in Hunter's, we got up and followed him through a series of doors until we reached Carter's bed. He was right, Carter was sound asleep.

"If there's a problem, let us know. For now we'll let him sleep and move him back to his room once he wakes up and we make sure all his vitals are good," he walked out and shut the curtain behind him.

"Why don't you two head out to lunch?" Mom suggested a couple minutes later.

"Are you sure?" I didn't want to leave Carter. Not now, not ever.

"I'm positive. He's just sleeping. By the time you get back he'll probably be awake," she knew I needed the change in scenery.

"Okay," I looked up at Hunter, "You ready then?"

"Yep," he said, smiling at me.

"See you later, I'll be back soon."

We walked out of the room, down the hall, and to the lobby.

The walk to his car in the parking deck was a quiet one, the kind of quiet that says, *I'll listen whenever you're ready.* We reached his car and he opened the door for me, waiting until I was seated to shut the door. He walked around and took the driver's seat, starting the engine.

"So, how are you?" We sat in the quiet of the parking deck at the hospital, his eyes resting intently on me, something I couldn't remember seeing for a long time.

"Better than yesterday, I guess."

83

"Good," he said, "So let's get your mind off of this. Let's talk about New York."

New York? That was the last possible thing on my mind. The thought of leaving Carter was unbearable.

"Okay, what about it?"

"What about it? Is this coming from the girl who hasn't stopped talking about New York since freshman year?"

I just laughed, enjoying the time with him that for months I had hoped for. As he drove I couldn't help but wonder if this loving attitude would last more than a couple days or weeks.

"I've heard it's really fun to get ice cream, sit in Times Square and people watch. We could do that one day," he said.

"Sounds really romantic and not creepy at all." Sarcasm rang in my tone.

"Hey, I'm just throwing out suggestions! Do you have any better ones?"

"Well, we could go to Carlos' bakery, you know the guy from Cake Boss. We could go to the Metropolitan Museum of Art, and we have to visit Madison Square Garden."

"An art museum? That's way too educational for a fun trip together!"

We laughed and kept talking about all the fun, and not so fun things to do in NY, as we drove through downtown to our favorite diner.

Chapter 8

Mom met me in the lobby that afternoon after lunch and led me to Carter's room. He looked physically and emotionally exhausted even in his sleep; sort of like he'd been run over, *oh wait, he had.*

We sat and talked for a little while before the doctor came in. With the creak of the door Carter woke up and saw me in the room.

"You're back," he gave me a weak smile before turning his attention to the doctor.

"Good afternoon," the doctor said coming in, directing his next question at Carter, "Now, from my understanding you work abroad?"

Creeper, how did he know that? I thought.

"Yes sir."

"And you understand it will be quite a while before you can return?"

He took a deep breath as his face dropped and then answered, "Yes sir."

The anger rose again in my chest. *God, all he wants is to serve you. You're stopping him from doing even that.*

"I'm very sorry, son," he said seeing his crushed expression and patting Carter on the shoulder before saying, "I will be checking back in with you all in just a few hours."

I walked up to Carter's bed and just sat beside him as a couple tears fell silently down his cheeks. All I could picture was the light in his eyes every time he told a story or showed us a picture. That passion he had for spreading the love of Jesus to the people in Uganda resonated in his body even as he lay on the hospital bed, broken that he couldn't return. We all sat quietly and looked anxiously at him, knowing there really wasn't much we could do.

The next day I volunteered to stay with Carter while everyone else went home for a couple of hours. Texting Hunter, I sat thinking about the last week and the past few days I'd spent with him. I was worried about him, but those past couple of days, with just the two of us, it was much more normal. Before that, he hadn't really seemed much like himself, always stressed out, not wanting to spend a lot of time together. I was beyond thankful for the normalcy that had occurred within those past few days, even the past twenty-four hours. When I thought about the rest of my life? That was a different story.

"So, we haven't really talked since," Carter said unexpectedly. I had no idea he was awake.

"Since I got you crushed in the car accident," I interrupted.

He gave me that look like, *you are being ridiculous, can't we just talk?*

"How are you feeling?" I asked him.

"Fine, I guess."

"Are you still on that pain medication?"

"Of course, the accident was only yesterday, Chrissy." He meant it jokingly, but at this point, nothing was really funny.

"I know, and I'm really sorry."

"Sorry for what? You didn't cause the wreck. That car hit us," he said, as I went and sat beside him on the hospital bed and told me what I had already heard a million times.

"The doctor said that if you wouldn't have leaned over to protect me that your leg and foot may not have been broken."

"But he also said something worse could have happened if I hadn't," he said almost in a reprimanding tone.

"You heard all of that?"

"Yep."

"Oh."

"Chrissy, I will be fine. I'm just glad you are okay," he said looking me in the eyes.

"I know you will, but you look so broken."

"My brokenness will heal over time."

"Carter, what can I do for you?" I asked desperately.

"I want you to..." He paused taking a deep breath, his eyes scanning the sterile hospital room.

"Want me to, what?" I pleaded, and suddenly realized that this was going to be more than going to get him a bag of peanut M&M's and a Diet Coke.

"I want you to go to Jinja, Uganda and help Rob and Amber with the Sole Hope project I was supposed to help with, and stay for six weeks. They need one more pair of hands."

"What?" I asked incredulously. My eyes widened and I had to stop myself from letting my mouth hang open. I was shocked to say the least.

"I want you to go to Uganda for six weeks," he spelled it out for me.

"I understood that, but..."

"But you asked me what you could do for me, and since I can't go back for at least a few months, if not more because of surgery, I want you to go in my place."

I took a deep breath, finally grasping what he wanted me to do and said, "I'll do it, but just for you."

"Good, that's settled," he said with a bemused smile, turning the TV on.

I'm going to have to get money, because they will not transfer tickets from Carter's name to mine. And Uganda?!? That is all the way across the world. This is SO not my thing, why did I just agree to that? I thought. Carter pretended to be completely oblivious to my shock

88

and just kept watching ESPN with a smug look on his face.

When Mom, Dad, and Carly walked in about an hour later Carter welcomed them by saying, "Chrissy is going to Uganda for six weeks!"

"What did you just say?" Mom asked walking up to me.

"Chrissy," Carter looked at me, implying that I was supposed to explain the rest.

"Well, I asked Carter what I could do for him. Since he can't go back for a while, he told me he wanted me to go to Uganda and help Rob and Amber with the Sole Hope project they are going to be a part of and stay for six weeks. I said yes."

"Has the doctor said how long it will be before you can go back? I mean, yesterday he said it would be a while, but has he given you a time frame?" Mom asked compassionately, not even thinking about the fact that she might be letting her seventeen year old daughter go to a foreign country, by herself, for over a month.

"Not exactly, but I'm going to ask him next time he comes in." Carter replied.

"How are you going to get the money for this?" Dad asked, changing the subject. I could tell he was not in favor of the whole thing, in fact, I was pretty sure no one was but Carter.

"I have no idea," I replied, but then Carly, being the genius, big-mouthed, older sister that she is, said, "Weren't you going to go on that trip to New York with your class this summer? How much had you saved for that?"

"Almost a thousand dollars, but I doubt that would be enough," I told her.

"If you went through the right airlines and asked for the humanitarian relief rate it would definitely be enough. Don't you think?" Carter proposed.

"That could work," Dad was weighing the idea but I couldn't really read his expression.

"Wait, wouldn't she just have to transfer the ticket?" Carter asked, quickly changing the subject.

"Yeah, I guess that's all. So a thousand would more than cover it. But I don't think money is really the issue here," Dad said.

"I agree, do you think you could handle it, honey?" Mom asked concerned.

"I know she can," Carter threw in.

"*I* don't know," I said, putting my hands in my face. I sat down hard on the sofa, once again wondering what in the world I had just agreed to. When we got home that night I practically stumbled up the stairs. I lay in bed for a while, trying to comprehend that I was more than likely going to be in Africa in two weeks. Thoughts were flying through my head, *I'll miss my trip to New York. They will all be basking in the glory of Broadway lights, while my feet are getting covered with dirt. Why am I doing this? Not to mention the fact that I'm leaving Carter here, broken.*

"Good morning, Mom," I said cheerfully as I headed downstairs the next morning. I had every intention of telling her that I changed my mind about going to Uganda, that I had made a quick decision; the wrong decision.

"Good morning, you're in a good mood," she replied. She quickly changed her tone, "I really want to talk to you about going to Uganda."

"Yeah, me too."

"What do you think about it?"

"I already told Carter I would, but I don't know," she stopped me very quickly.

"It means a lot to him to get this Sole Hope thing started."

"I don't know if I can do it though." I heard some whining in my voice.

"Which one, missing New York, or going to Africa?" She asked bluntly.

I hesitated, hating to face the truth.

"Both. I really want to go on my trip, and it kind of scares me, you know, going by myself."

"Chrissy, you were going to go to New York without your family, and I know you want to go on that trip, but I feel that this would be really good for you right now."

What could I say to that? She had just pretty much told me I was going.

"I have faith that you can do this. Your dad and I talked last night and we both agreed that we think you should go. Plus, your brother is really counting on you."

91

"I still don't necessarily *want* to go, but I will. For Carter," I said, trudging back up the stairs; that good attitude she had talked about? Yeah... it was gone.

"Good! We will book your tickets in the next few days."

"Okay," I said, slamming my door, throwing myself on my bed. I was not at all thrilled about this trip or missing my trip to New York.

Chapter 9

A couple days later things seemed to be calming down a bit. Mom and Dad were back at work. Carly and I spent most days with Carter at the hospital, making him laugh and drawing on his face while he was asleep. We may have even painted his toenails one day; shows how mature we really are.

"Do you know how to transfer plane tickets? Mom said I needed to figure all that out this week," I asked him while we watched re-runs of sitcoms on TV one day.

"Yep, bring me my laptop and we can do it now." I brought him his computer and sat down beside him on the bed. We found a travel website and after an hour of frustrating phone calls and emails, the tickets had been transferred. In exactly a week, at 6:30 am, I would be leaving for Uganda in Carter's place.

"You will have to get there no later than 4:30 in order to go through security and get to your terminal in time. I also need you to email Rob and Amber telling them you are coming. I already told them that I had gotten hurt in a car wreck, but they didn't think anyone would be coming in my place."

All of this left butterflies in my stomach and I felt like I could throw-up all over the hospital room. Carter handed me his laptop after he pulled up his email. I started typing, trying to be careful not to say anything about how badly I did *not* want to be going and how much I would much rather be in New York. The email finally read:

Dear Rob and Amber,

This is Chrissy, Carter's little sister. Since Carter will not be able to come back to Uganda and work on the project, he has requested for me to come and stay for six weeks, helping you all out. I am leaving one week from today, at 6:30 am. I can't wait to see you all again.

Love,
Chrissy

The rest of the day wasn't very exciting. Carter rested a lot which was typical. We were all beyond thankful that was his last full day at the hospital. Mom and Dad brought Chick-Fil-A for dinner since we all needed something other than cafeteria food. At about 7:00pm that night, we heard a knock at the door.

"Come in," Dad said, and Carter's doctor came in.

"How are you feeling?" he asked Carter.

"All right, my foot is still pretty painful, but my leg is just sore."

94

"Well, that's to be expected, so I am going to send some pain meds and antibiotics home with you. You will need to come back once the swelling goes down to get a hard cast on your leg."

"Okay."

"Here is a packet of information on how to take care of him once you get home." He handed Mom a packet of information that looked like a dictionary; it was that big. This whole conversation reminded me of how guilty I still felt for all of this.

"Thanks," Mom responded. I could tell she was overwhelmed by all of it. She wasn't the one who needed to be overwhelmed since Carly and I would be the ones taking care of him for while!

"I'll be back first thing in the morning to check in on you and make sure it will be okay for you to go home."

"Thank you for everything," Dad said as the doctor walked out the room.

"I'm so glad I get to go home," Carter said after he walked out, breathing a sigh of relief.

"Me too, I'm tired of this place," I said, and everybody laughed. That night Mom stayed with Carter while Dad, Carly and I headed home. It was hard to leave Carter at the hospital every night, but there was nothing like crawling into my own bed after a long day at the hospital. When I got into bed, my phone rang.

"Hey Hunter," I said.

"Hey, how are you?"

"Good, I guess."

"What's wrong?"

"For one thing, I'm not going on the trip to New York, and two my brother has a broken leg and a crushed foot."

"So it's official?" He asked.

"What?"

"You're going to Uganda?" His voice held an unexpected frustration.

"Yep. I'm missing New York, Broadway, Gucci; everything."

"I still don't think it's safe for you to go by yourself. Besides, New York won't be any fun without you."

I sighed as I finally laid my head down on my pillow." I'm going to be staying with a couple that goes to our church, the only time I'll be by myself is on the plane. I'll be all right. Trust me, I don't want to go. I'm only doing it for Carter."

"Then tell him that you don't want to go," he said this like it was no big deal. He didn't have any siblings, I didn't expect him to know how I felt.

"I can't, Hunter. I was driving the car, he protected me and then ended up not being able to walk for a long time; I have to do this for him."

"All right."

"I know it's no fun, but I'll go, get it over with and come back. I'll still be the same Chrissy."

"That's true. Well, I better go, Mom needs to ask me something, probably has to do with the divorce and all that fun stuff."

"I'm sorry."

"It's okay, love you."

"I love you, too." With this we hung up and I closed my eyes, my mind still spinning.

The next day Mom and Dad took the day off from work so they could help get Carter home and settled in. We all got to the hospital about 9:00am, and to our surprise the doctor was already there talking to them.

"Good morning," the doctor said as we walked in, "I have checked on Carter and it seems that he will be just fine to go on home."

"Awesome," I said with a grin.

"He will be on bed rest for at least the next month and then after that he will have to take it easy for quite a long while as he may or may not be able to walk on his own. He will have to begin physical therapy next week after he is placed in a hard cast. I told him he will have to wait at least three months before returning."

"Okay," Dad said disappointedly.

"Let's see, it's Tuesday, so I will schedule him an appointment next Tuesday to get hard casts on his leg. Then in about six weeks, if there are no complications, come back to get them removed. After that we will move on to physical therapy," he said handing Mom a piece of paper with even more information on it.

"Thank you," she responded, "For everything."

"The nurses will be here in about thirty minutes to help him get checked out of the hospital."

"Thank you," we all responded as he walked out.

"Three months," Carter said to himself rubbing his forehead with his strong hands.

"I know that's a long time, but he wants you completely healed before you return," Mom said, walking to his bed putting an arm around his shoulders.

"I guess that would be important. Good thing Chrissy is going for a while."

"Yep," I said, once again contemplating my decision.

Half an hour later two nurses came and wheeled Carter out of the hospital. Dad helped him into the front seat of the Tahoe, and everybody else hopped in the back. As we drove down the road to our house, the beautiful blue skies and white puffy clouds I saw overhead did not match my mood or the feeling in my heart. I wanted my life back to normal. I wanted to be going to New York. But most of all I wanted Carter back to the way he was. With the help of his wheelchair, we got Carter inside and helped him onto the brown leather couch where he would hang out for the next month. Then I sat down in the chair beside him and made him tell me a bunch of information I would need for my quickly approaching trip to Uganda.

"Will they be doing church planting work while I'm there?"

"Not while we are doing everything with Sole Hope, no. They are going to focus on that for a couple of months since they've got several churches grounded and growing. The only thing they'll be doing is going out every couple of days to check up on the various church sites."

98

"Okay, so what will I need to bring?"

"You will need clothes of course, I usually wore khakis and a t-shirt, but you will have to wear a skirt that reaches to your knees, at least. You will definitely want tennis shoes, or some sort of closed toed shoes. You will also need sun screen and lots of it. Let's see, shampoo, conditioner, and whatever else you girls need in the bathroom. My room has its own small bathroom. You won't need blankets or sheets, those are all in my room already," he said, and I mentally wrote it all down.

"So pretty much everything I would need if I went to New York?"

"Chrissy, I know you don't really want to go, but I think you will learn so much and that you will come out of all of this and have had a great time. Most importantly, I think you will grow spiritually. The Lord has a way of grabbing ahold of your heart when you're serving Him twenty four-seven. This will be so much more rewarding than anything Gucci could ever give you. With that being said, I am sorry you have to miss your trip to New York, though."

"Well at least someone knows how I feel," I murmured underneath my breath.

"Chrissy, I always know how you feel," he said having heard me.

"That's pretty much why I'm going."

"I can't even tell you how much I appreciate this."

"I think I can imagine."

"I don't think you can," he said, and our conversation ended when his computer beeped signaling he had an email from Rob and Amber.

Dear Chrissy,
Rob and I can't tell you how much we appreciate you coming to Uganda to help us. This is such a blessing and we can't wait to see you. Make sure Carter tells you everything you need to bring and how to prepare. See you soon- thanks again.
In His love,
Amber

"You are doing a really good thing, Chrissy."

"Thanks," I said.

"Oh, I meant to tell you I got in contact with one of the girls who works with Sole Hope. She's my age and came home about two weeks ago to visit with family before returning for the summer. They only live about an hour away and it just so happens that she's going to be on the same flight as you."

"Really?" I asked, though I could see exactly where he was going with this.

"So, I gave her your number and told her to text you. I thought maybe ya'll could meet up in the airport and hopefully sit together on the plane. She's really awesome, her name's Paige. I have a feeling ya'll will be good friends."

"That's cool. What's her number? I'll go ahead and put it in my phone." I pulled my phone from my pocket and opened my contacts, typing *Paige.* Carter used his phone and gave me her number.

"I figured you might want some kind of connection before going," he put his phone away and looked at me.

"Thanks."

He was trying to make this a fun trip, one that would somehow be better than a week in New York City. Even though I really did appreciate all he was doing to make me feel more comfortable, I knew it wouldn't be as amazing as he thought it would. But I didn't want to let him down, so I figured I should at least try, too.

With this, I walked up to my bedroom to make a packing list. Heading into my bedroom, I overheard my sister on the phone.

"Thanks for calling, I'll talk to you tomorrow," she said.

I plopped down on her bed and sat down beside her.

"What's up? You okay?" She was all choked up, but I knew it was probably nothing more than her being her normal drama queen self.

"Nathan is just so sweet."

"What happened?"

"He has called almost every day to check on Carter and see if we need anything, which doesn't really make any sense since he lives like three hours away, but whatever. He's just being so sweet and concerned about everything."

"Awwww, how sweet," I said giggling.

"Anyway, do you need help with a packing list?" She playfully slapped me on the arm.

"Actually, that would be great. Let me go get my New York list and we can revise that one." I returned moments later with my well thought out list that was perfectly equipped for everything a girl might need in the Big Apple.

One by one, things were crossed off; things that were unnecessary to have in Uganda. Jewelry to go with every planned outfit, half a dozen pairs of shoes, and two or three purses wouldn't be needed. They were replaced with bug spray, sunscreen, and enough hair ties to last a lifetime. Just looking at this list wasn't nearly as fun as seeing the one it had been just thirty minutes before.

In between a trip to Target and dinner as a family on Thursday, I got a text from Paige.

Hey Chrissy! This is Paige. I don't know if Carter has told you about me or not...but I thought maybe we could Skype for a little bit if that's okay.

I responded immediately, a little nervous to talk to her.

Hi! He has, actually. And Skyping sounds great.

She gave me her username and within minutes we were talking over the computer screen. When her face first came up on my screen, she smiled and her hazel colored eyes perfectly complemented the caramel-brown hair that fell to her shoulders.

"Hey!" She said waving.

"Hi!" I waved back.

"Carter's told me so much about you," she pulled her hair to one side of her face.

"I hope he only told the good stuff," I laughed.

"There were only a few stories that you might not appreciate," she laughed back.

"And these were?" I gave her a questioning glance.

"I think the first was when you were little and walked around the house dressed in a swimsuit, goggles and leg warmers," her laughter returned.

"I guess that one's not too bad!"

"But then one night while celebrating Rob and Amber's anniversary, he told us that when you guys went to Rob and Amber's wedding you tripped on the edge of your dress while dancing at the reception and totally busted on the dance floor."

"Okay, now that one's a little worse," I really laughed, picturing the memory in my head.

"Anyway, Carter wanted me to ask you about meeting up in the airport Monday morning," she changed the subject quickly. *I liked the stories better...thinking about Monday isn't fun at all.*

"That would be great. I've only flown once with my family so this will be a whole new experience," my stomach began to churn at the thought of maneuvering an airport on my own.

"It can be scary the first time, but I'm sure you'll be fine."

"Thanks," for the first time while talking about Uganda, I gave a real smile. Maybe Paige and I really would become friends.

"The chances of us making it through security at the same time are slim, so we can just meet at the terminal before boarding."

"That would be great."

"Your brother has told me a little bit of background about you coming."

I gave a sigh, not knowing how much she knew... wondering if she knew that I didn't want to be going.

"It's not going to be an easy trip, I can tell you that. You'll be working hard. I'm sure Carter has already told you this, but you'll see the Lord work some amazing things in and around us while you're there. By the end, you'll love it. I promise."

"Thanks," my nerves continued to grow as I sat talking to her.

"Well, I better go. I'm meeting some friends for dinner that I haven't seen since I left a year ago."

"Yeah, we're having dinner in just a few minutes," I glanced at the clock, surprised Mom hadn't called me down for dinner yet.

"I'll see you Monday, then," she gave another warm smile.

"Sounds good, and thanks again, Paige," I said.

"No problem! Bye!"

With that we both logged off. Even though for a moment Paige had made Uganda seem a little less scary,

I was still dreading Monday morning... the morning that, much to my dismay, was coming quicker than I had imagined.

Then the big day came. The day I would get on that airplane and fly halfway across the world *by. my. self.* Most of all I tried not to think about how I would be missing a trip to New York with all of my best friends and boyfriend.

Chapter 10

The clock read 3:30am. My alarm felt like it was ringing directly in my ear canal and I desperately desired sleep, more sleep. But, I was leaving for Africa that day. Going back to sleep wasn't an option. Crawling out of bed, I grabbed my clothes that I had set out the night before and hopped in the shower. Despite neglecting my relationship with God lately, I figured now would be as good a time as ever to rekindle. So, instead of my normal singing, I decided to utilize my time with prayer.

"God," I whispered, "It's been tough, and honestly I really don't want to do this. I don't know why you want me to do this or why you had any of this happen. So, I'm gonna need your help. Big time. I'm going to need patience and love and peace about my life in general. All of that would be great to have on this trip. Oh, and it would be really nice for Carter not to break anything else or get sick while I'm gone. Amen." With that I turned the water off and completed my morning routine- just a *little* earlier than normal.

"Are you ready, Chrissy?" Carter asked as I joined him on the couch.

"As ready as I'll ever be," I paused, "Do you really think I can do this?"

"I don't know if I've told you this, but when I went over there the first time I didn't know what to do with so many people around me. It was so evident that they all needed the Lord but I couldn't reach them all. But then I connected with just one young boy and from there I realized it only takes one life to make a difference. Just start with one. It doesn't seem nearly as hard that way."

"Thanks," I tried to listen to his advice but it just got mixed in with all of my nervous thoughts.

"I wish I could go to the airport with you," he said looking right at me.

"Me, too," I said in agreement.

"Don't forget, you won't be alone. Paige is meeting you at the terminal."

I nodded.

"Thanks again for doing this."

"You're welcome. You know, I wouldn't be going if it weren't you who needed me too."

Our tender conversation was interrupted.

"Chrissy, time to go," Mom shouted, and I walked over to Carter and gave him a hug.

"Love you, Chrissy. Be safe," he said hugging me back, I could hear the sadness in his voice, "Oh, I almost forgot. I have something for you." He leaned over and picked up a beautiful, leather bound journal off of the coffee table. On the front was an engraving- a quote he had lovingly selected just for me.

I am the daughter of a King who is not moved by the world. For my God is with me and goes before me. I do not fear because I am His.

My throat burned as I said, "Thanks Carter. It's beautiful."

Tears threatened to spill but I kept them in. I knew once I started there would be no going back.

"It's for you to journal in while you're gone. I had one when I went," he said. I leaned over and embraced him one last time.

"I'm going to miss you."

"I'll miss you, too. Love you, kiddo."

"Love you," I said walking out the door, my heart pounding, my stomach tying itself into a million knots. I had so many questions going through my mind, but tried to block them out and sing along to the music Mom and Dad had playing in the car.

"Girls, why don't you get on out and I'll go park the car," my dad said stopping the Tahoe at the airport entrance.

"You okay?" Carly asked, putting one arm around my shoulder.

I nodded with a deep breath as we rolled my luggage inside. I had paid the extra fifty dollars to be able to have another suitcase.

"Alright kiddo," my dad said after joining us inside at the check in gate, "You will have to go on from here by yourself."

"Okay." My eyes welled with tears and my voice was starting to crack. *I am* not *going to start crying again.*

"You will do awesome," Mom said as she hugged me tightly. I didn't want to let go.

"I love you. Skype us when you get there," Dad hugged me.

"Have a good trip," Carly said.

"I will, love you guys." I walked forward, beginning my adventure. At that moment I remembered that I could have been going to New York with my boyfriend and best friends- not to Uganda by myself. With these visions filling my head, I passed through security and sat waiting for the plane to board. I grabbed the travel journal Carter had given me, and wrote,

Monday, June 11th

Well, here I am. Waiting in the airport and I couldn't be more nervous, I'm pretty sure that I might throw up. I would much rather be going to New York in a few weeks, so I'm counting on God to do some miraculous things while I'm gone. I haven't really heard a word from Him about anything in a long time. This trip better be amazing.

"Chrissy!" I stood after hearing Paige's voice behind me. I waved as she walked up rolling one small suitcase behind her and a backpack slung over one shoulder.

She embraced me and put her stuff down beside mine.

"It's so good to meet you," she said as we sat down in the plastic airport chairs.

"I know," I had to agree with her. After our Skype conversation, meeting her was the only thing I was looking forward to.

"Are you nervous?" she asked.

"Very," I said laughing.

"Don't be. You've made it through the hardest part. Now, if you can get to sleep on the plane you'll be an expert traveler!"

"We will now begin boarding all passengers seated in rows twenty through forty," the attendant at the desk announced in her robotic voice.

Together Paige and I walked up to the counter, handed her our tickets and passports and she let us through to board the airplane. Though Paige didn't seem the least bit nervous, my head was spinning. I eventually found my seat near the window and put my huge lavender back-pack with my name embroidered on the pocket, under the seat in front of me. After a conversation with the older lady who was supposed to sit next to me, Paige sat down beside of me and made herself comfortable for our flight to Dulles International in Washington D. C. Paige pulled a magazine from her backpack and began to read. I sat, knees shaking as seat belts were checked and instructions were given.

Suddenly, I felt the plane start to shake. When I looked out the window we were moving. Then we lurched into the air. I could see my hometown getting smaller and smaller as we climbed, distance separating me from my small world below until finally, we were surrounded by clouds. A thought occurred to me while I took in the beauty of it all. *Would I have missed this? Flying to New York I would have been so preoccupied with my friends... I would have missed it.*

"So, besides nervous, how are you?" Paige looked at me and I could tell that she really wanted to know. I contemplated telling her how I really felt. If she and Carter were friends I figured I could trust her. Plus, something about her made it easy to carry a conversation, something I wasn't normally good at with new people.

"Honestly?" I looked at her imploringly.

"Absolutely."

"I'm actually missing a trip to New York with my class so I can go for Carter."

"Really?" her eyes widened.

"Yeah."

"I'm guessing you're not too pumped, then?"

"Not at all," something in me felt bad for even saying this.

"You want to know something?" she paused." When I went on my first trip to Africa in tenth grade I was completely dreading it, much like I think you are."

111

I nodded, "So what made you want to work in Uganda with Sole Hope?"

"The story is rather lengthy, but we certainly have the time," I nodded in agreement. "My parents wanted all of us to take a family trip to visit a missionary family from our church during my sophomore year of high school. It was only a two week trip, but I was mad because we were going to be missing all of Christmas break.

"While we were there, the Lord convicted me about the way I had been living and treating others. I wasn't the nicest teenager on the planet. I can't really explain it, you know, what happened over there. When we got back to the States, I changed my habits and my life. Slowly but surely the Lord placed calling on me to serve Him in Africa. "Right after I decided to pursue the mission field, my dad found out he had pancreatic cancer. I was so confused. I mean, the Lord had just shown me so clearly what He wanted me to do with my life. But then the lines were blurred and the biggest obstacle imaginable arose."

"Oh my word. I'm so sorry," I felt so badly for her.

"Thanks. I figured it probably wouldn't be the best time to tell him my newly found calling for life. Especially since I'm the only girl in the family."

"I couldn't imagine being the only girl."

She laughed and then continued, "Anyway, I figured I would wait until he was somewhat better to tell him what I had decided." With this Paige sighed, paused and stared at the floor, "But he never got better. It only got worse. He struggled with it for almost two years, and it was the hardest two years of my life. Right before he passed away he told all of us that he wanted us to go to college, no matter what. After that, he wanted us to do whatever God was calling us to do, so that's what I did. I went to college at Appalachian State, and then applied to go to Uganda through Sole Hope. Now I'm on my way back from a break visiting family and couldn't be more thrilled about what I do."

"That's crazy," I said shocked at how everything had played out in her life.

"It's amazing to look back and see how God was weaving every part of it, too. On some of those days when he was in hospice, I thought that it would never end, that things would never return to the way they were before. Even though it's not the same without him, God is always faithful. He keeps His promises when we keep our faith in Him." By this point we had already made the switch in D.C. to the plane that would carry us over the ocean to Amsterdam where we would make another switch and fly the last leg to Uganda.

I was so very glad I had found someone to and talk to on the long flight there. Many, many hours passed. It was over eighteen hours total. Very few of them were spent in sleep, in fact, most of them were spent talking with Paige about life stories, interests and life in Uganda. I was grateful to have gotten to know her on the first flight because when we switched planes in Dulles and then in Amsterdam she knew what she was doing. Twice we were able to trade seats with someone and sit together on the next flights.

Day and night were confused by the time we neared Uganda. The flight attendants once again came around the plane and reminded everyone to fasten their seat belts. We came to a screeching halt and a resounding thud on the ground. While picking my backpack off the floor of the plane I said to Paige, "I'm really glad we got to sit together. I don't know how I would have done it without you."

"Absolutely! Normally my flights are so boring, I've enjoyed spending this time with you," she said back. After walking off of the plane, we got our suitcases from the baggage claim area and I remembered that Carter had told me that Rob and Amber would be waiting for me at the airport; he was right.

"Chrissy, Paige, over here!" they shouted, holding up a sign that said, *"Welcome to Uganda, Chrissy!"* and together Paige and I walked over to them with our bags in hand.

It took a minute for me to recognize them. Amber's hair had been cut into a short bob the last time I'd seen her. She now had her long locks pulled into a thick side braid. Rob's beard was longer than the last time I'd seen him and his shaved head had grown out as well.

"I didn't get a sign?" Paige said with sarcastic offense in her voice, "Feelin' the love, guys." We all laughed as Rob loaded our bags onto a rolling luggage cart.

"How was your flight?" Amber asked.

"It was much better than I thought it would be," I said truthfully.

"Carter got the two of us in contact before coming here. It made my flight much more enjoyable to have someone to talk to," Paige said.

As we stepped out of the airport doors, I was greeted by the overwhelming heat. *And I thought summers in North Carolina were hot,* I thought to myself. Next I took in the smell and everything I saw. It smelled smoky, like a mix of burning wood and dust along with the faintest hint of fresh fruit. In front of me were more mountains than I could count. Villages were scattered underneath them just miles away from me.

Even after seeing Carter's pictures, my immediate thought of Africa was still a bare, dry and hot place, one that certainly would not be beautifully appointed with mountains and trees.

"Chrissy, you have really grown up since we have seen you last," Amber said as we were driving down the road.

"Thanks," I guess. I readjusted my ponytail only to find my hair greasy and tangled from the flight over. *What I would do for a hot shower right now?* I couldn't help but think.

"How is Carter doing?" Rob asked. I told them about his condition and how he would not be able to return for at least three months. I was exhausted after traveling for nearly twenty-four hours. I had just flown half way across the world for my big brother. I didn't want to be there.

If I don't get some good sleep soon...

"Well, here it is!" Amber said, pulling up to the missionary guest house after quickly dropping Paige off at the Sole Hope compound. The house was larger than I had pictured, but I had forgotten that they hosted missionaries all the time, "Come on, we'll go in the back door."

Rob got my suitcases out of the back and we walked in the back door. We stepped into the kitchen and my eyes swept the room. Pictures of family and friends hung on the refrigerator and a table with four chairs sat in the kitchen. In the adjoining room, there was a huge table with a long bench on either side." This is the kitchen, and that's the dining room. Nothing fancy, just a big table!" Amber said laughing.

"Here's the living room. I'm not really sure why we have a TV, since it hasn't been turned on in over a year, and when it's used we just watch movies," she said as we walked in to a large room with a cream colored sectional on one side of the room and a love seat on the other. Gray walls and wood flooring further enhanced the sun shining into the room. The space was airy and bright, the fans spinning above my head created a fresh breeze in the room despite the lack of air conditioning.

Leaving the living room Rob said, "This is one of the guest rooms, and here is the downstairs bathroom." He showed me a bedroom with a bunk that had a double bed on the bottom and a twin on top. The adjoining bathroom was just big enough to have a shower, toilet and sink.

"Let's grab your stuff and head on upstairs," Amber said.

"Sounds good." I slung my bag on my back and walked upstairs, thankful that Rob had volunteered to lug my suitcase up the steps.

"Here we are," Amber said, "Your suite. Oh, and the hot water situation is a little iffy. An electric heater warms the water. It takes about twenty minutes and once the water runs out, it's out for a while. Sometimes, it just doesn't work and our only explanation is that it's Uganda. So you may or may not have hot water." She gave a small laugh.

And there went hopes for a hot shower.

"Anyway, make yourself at home. Dinner will be ready soon!" She said.

"Alright, thanks."

They both walked downstairs and I was left to take it all in.

The bedroom was painted cream, it had a striped blue and green bedspread on the bed, and the cement floors were covered by a navy blue rug... it reminded me so much of Carter. There was a wooden desk across the room from the bed and dresser, into which I put all of my clothes. After arranging my things, I explored a bit upstairs. I didn't find anything out of the ordinary, just another guest bedroom and Rob and Amber's bedroom.

117

I sat down on the edge of the bed and thought, *well, this is home.*

And for the first time the fact that I really was in Uganda felt real.

About an hour later, I hesitantly made my way downstairs to see what was for dinner.

"Hey! Do you like fish? I made fresh tilapia for dinner."

I nodded with a fake smile on my face. I had never tried a fish that I enjoyed.

"Here's your plate," she handed me a plate with a piece of fish on it.

"And there are chips and fresh guacamole on the counter, help yourself!" She fixed plates for herself and Rob as I fixed my own.

"In the morning I'll make passion fruit juice, it's delicious."

"Sounds good," I sat down at the table and waited for Rob and Amber to join me at the small table in the kitchen before trying the fish.

"Let's pray," Rob stated, sitting down and bowing his head,

"Lord, we thank You for this beautiful night and for bringing Chrissy and Paige here safely. We pray for Carter's healing and ask that you would be with their entire family. We thank you for your unconditional love and the amazing plans you have for all of us. We love you, Lord. It's in your name we pray, amen."

"Amen," Amber echoed.

Dinner conversation focused on explanations of the city of Jinja, where they lived, church planting projects and the work Sole Hope was doing all over Uganda. *I just want some sleep. I've barely slept in twenty four hours,* I thought, swallowing another bite of tilapia, which to my surprise wasn't half bad. After dinner we played cards for a while before I headed up to my room.

"Don't forget to use the mosquito net hanging above your bed!" Amber reminded me as I walked up to my room.

"Thanks," I replied.

I couldn't help but try and skype Hunter. I was already homesick. A few minutes later, we were talking to each other over the computer screen. I was relieved to see a familiar face.

"So how's it going?" He asked me.

"Pretty good. Not New York, though."

"I know. How was your flight?"

"Long, but I met up with the girl Carter knew from Uganda and she was really awesome, we talked the entire way over."

"That's neat," his expression was blank.

"How are your parents?"

"Fine, Dad's trying to file paperwork to make the separation official. I'm just trying to stay out of it."

"I'm so sorry."

"It's okay."

"So," I stopped when I heard something from his side of the computer.

"Hunter, we need to go," I heard his mom yell.

"All right, I've got to go, then," we said our goodbyes and I tucked myself in. The conversation with Hunter had been rather emotionless, certainly not bringing the sense of home I had been hoping for.

Tuesday, June 12th

Well, I'm here. I'm in Uganda. It feels very surreal to be in all the same places that I saw in Carter's pictures. I sat beside Carter's friend, Paige on the planes and she was so awesome. I'm hoping to get to spend some time with her while I'm here. Oh! And I ate tilapia today. Mom will be so proud of me for trying new foods. Anyway. These last twenty four hours have been non-stop. I'm exhausted. And hot...very hot. Goodnight.

Lying in bed, I threw off the blankets as they were entirely too heavy for this warm Ugandan night. Though the fan created a nice breeze, it was impossible to lie still enough to sleep with the mosquito net hanging above my head. As I willed myself to fall asleep, I thought about the last twenty four hours: the plane ride, the conversations with Paige, the fact that I had actually eaten tilapia...that less than two months ago this was Carter's room. I wrestled with these thoughts and struggled to fall asleep until one in the morning, I finally dozed off.

Chapter 11

"Good morning," Amber said peeking her head in the door, waking me up with the creaking of the door.

"Morning," I said rolling over, wishing I could sleep another five hours.

"Why don't you come on downstairs for breakfast?"

I nodded and she walked out. Within three minutes, I was out of bed, changed, had my hair up, and was going downstairs in record time.

"How did you sleep last night?" Amber asked me when I walked in the kitchen.

"Great, sorry I slept so late." I went and pulled out a chair beside her.

"It's perfectly okay. There are Cheerios in the pantry, bowls in that cabinet there," she said, directing me to the pantry and a cabinet beside the sink, while simultaneously scanning the book in her hand, "and milk is in the fridge along with that fresh passion fruit juice I promised last night."

"Thanks," I said, going to the pantry and pulling out the Cheerios. Once I fixed my cereal, I sat down with Amber and we talked while I ate.

"Can you believe that cheerios cost almost six dollars here?" Amber said.

"That's crazy!" I responded.

"Yeah, that's normally why we eat eggs and fruit for breakfast, but we figured you'd probably like something a little homier for your first little while."

I couldn't help but smile...they were trying so hard.

"What are you reading?" I asked. She had put her book down on the table when I sat down across from her.

"*One Thousand Gifts* by Ann Voskamp, I'll let you borrow it once I'm finished. It's really good so far. It is really making me aware of every gift I receive from God every day, the small and the large. As I see each gift and record it in my journal, I just feel thankfulness welling up inside. Such an amazing way to find joy in each day."

After that, conversation was minimal during breakfast since my scarce amount of sleep that night hadn't done much for me. After eating, we went to the orphanage to meet Rob. We passed several stores and so many mopeds. I could not believe how many people could be squeezed onto such a small seal. People passed us and I tried to take it all in. There was so much to see, such color, such beauty. Off in the distance mountains towered over little huts and teeny, tiny people. In front of me women passed us with baskets on their heads, holding the hands of small children with deep brown eyes, constantly glancing curiously at my white skin.

We were greeted at the orphanage by a tall, rickety blue metal gate. Brick walls surrounding the orphanage had shards of glass stuck in the top. Once inside the gate, about a dozen kids came running up to us. I guessed visitors were a big deal.

"Come on, I'll show you around," Amber said walking down the steps to the orphanage. My heart was struck with a devastating sense of heaviness as we entered the main hallway. The barren walls were painted a cream color with no art work whatsoever. Doors lined the walls on either side and nannies bustled back and forth from room to room carrying dirty laundry.

"Mostly pre-mature infants or sick babies stay in this room, and only a few certain nannies are allowed in here," she said as we passed a room with about ten cribs in it. I looked in the window of the shut door to see all the cribs, each of which had at least two tiny crying babies in them. They looked so helpless, so pitiful. Next we passed by a larger room, with twenty or so cribs in it.

"This is the room for the healthy babies, they stay in here until they are walking, then they move to this room, and sleep here until they are three years old." The room she referenced was exactly the same as the last. There were two more rooms, one for the three to four year olds and one for the four to five year olds. Each of these had lots of small beds, little toddler sized cribs that were old and worn, the bare walls and bare floors did not do much to add warmth. The only other rooms in the building, except for storage, were two larger rooms with long, low tables on each side and a bench for the children to sit on. This was where all the kids gathered to eat.

"Wait," a thought occurred to me, "Where are all of the kids?"

"They're outside playing," she said smiling.

"Okay, I was really confused for a minute."

"You're good. Here's our last stop," she said taking me back to a small room with mounds of boxes and bags. I was completely overwhelmed by my surroundings.

"Your brother probably told you about some of the things we will be doing. Starting in a couple of days, we will be hosting jigger clinics with Sole Hope. We have met with the founders, Dru and Asher Collie, a couple times to talk about specifics. We're thinking about beginning after breakfast and then working until early afternoon, or until people stop coming if it's before that. Then we will stay here and play with the children in the home. Since it's your first day here, you can just get to know some of the kids a bit."

"Sounds good!"

The rest of the day was spent playing with the children outside on their playground, a sad couple of swings and a single lonely slide. Many of the little girls took turns holding onto my pale hands, guiding me around the compound. The little boys kicked a beat-up soccer ball around us, each trying to out-do one another, vying for my attention. I could not get enough of them all. The day flew by and at five we headed back to the house to have dinner. After we had enjoyed a chicken and veggie stir-fry for dinner, I went up to my room and opened my laptop. I found an email from Carter!

Hey Chrissy!

I hope that you had a good flight there. We are all praying that you stay safe and are having a good trip. Tell me about everything you did today. Praying you will be able to hear from God. The house is quiet without you. Write back.

Love you -Carter

I responded, telling him all about my day and the flight there. I wrote a few short sentences about all of the kids I had seen that day and what we were planning to do in the next few days...how surreal it felt to be in the same places his pictures had been taken. When I had pressed send, I saw I also had an email from Hunter that I hadn't noticed before.

Chrissy,

I'm already missing you since talking last night. New York is quickly approaching and I still can't believe you're not coming. Anyway, stay safe. I can't wait for you to be back home so we can enjoy a little bit of summer together. Write back soon. Skype me whenever you can.

Love, Hunter

I crawled into bed without responding, I knew another morning would be upon me sooner than I desired. When I closed my eyes, all I could think about was Broadway in New York, and how much I wished I was home. I hadn't thought about it all day until Hunter mentioned it in his email. Just thinking about the lights, the music, the fancy hotels, and all of the shops made me devastated I wasn't going to be in New York with the rest of my class in just a few short days. Sleep refused to come so I turned on the lamp, and opened my journal to jot down my thoughts.

Wednesday, June 13th
So, it's been a busy day, and jet lag has really caught up with me, bringing my exhaustion to a whole new level. We went to the orphanage and Amber gave me a
"grand tour." It's certainly not New York. But to my own surprise, when I was at the orphanage I wasn't thinking of New York. I was thinking of those kids...those little girls and boys. Even after seeing Carter's pictures, it was still such a shock to see things as they actually are. Two and three year olds have to share a toddler sized bed. They are probably thankful to have a bed to sleep in at all. The conditions are so much sadder than I thought.
Standing among those kids today I felt so inadequate. What am I really doing here? Carter is so

close to the Lord yet I'm here doing the work he was supposed to be doing.

Speaking of Carter, I wonder how he is really feeling. How much pain he is in...I worry about him and think about him all the time. That and Broadway. The end - for today.

The next morning, I got up without Amber having to come remind me. I had hoped that a good night's sleep would bring refreshment but one night didn't cure the jet lag that was still hanging on. It was 7:30am Ugandan time, so I didn't think Hunter would be able to skype, but I gave it a try anyway. I just needed a little bit of home.

"Hey, Chrissy," Hunter said tiredly when he answered.

"Hey, how was your day?"

"Good, Josh and Matt came over, we played Modern Warfare II. I just fell asleep a little bit ago. How has your day been?"

"Well, it's only 7:30 here, but yesterday we went to the orphanage. Their conditions are devastating. I had seen Carter's pictures, but it's still so different in person. They have to share beds and the only attention they're getting is from the nannies, which is great, but it's not like the love of a family. The craziest thing is that these kids are so content, it really amazes me."

"Cool."

"Um, are you getting excited for New York?"

"Why are you bringing this up? Aren't you depressed about it? I know I would be."

127

"Yeah, sort of."

"Sort of? I know you are."

I just laughed, "I still want you to be excited."

"Thanks." Hunter must have realized what time it was. He turned back to me, rubbing his forehead in exhaustion." Listen, I better go. It's about 12:30. Love you."

"Love you too, talk to you tomorrow." *Well, that was short. Nothing like a two second Skype with your boyfriend,* I thought. *He's just tired,* I reassured myself.

After I had gotten dressed and eaten breakfast we walked over to the orphanage. On our way over they told me a few things about it.

"Yesterday you probably saw that this orphanage only has kids from newborns to age five. There is another orphanage that keeps all of the children older than this, much like a boarding school. They had to separate the ages mainly because of space. At some point over the next couple of weeks we have some adoptive families coming to pick up their children. It will be very exciting for the little ones, but it will also be hard for the rest of the kids, because they really won't know what is going on," Rob told me.

"What about the sibling groups? Will they get adopted together?" I asked.

"It just depends on the situation. They always try to keep them together," Amber replied. When we walked into the home, I saw Paige.

"Chrissy!" She exclaimed as we walked in.

"Hey Paige!" She embraced me with a hug.

"How are you?"

"A little tired, but good!"

"I bet. Well, Dru and Asher are actually here so you'll get to meet them this morning." We all walked back to the storage room, where we were surrounded by dozens of boxes filled with supplies for the Sole Hope clinics. Paige explained to us that each bin contained supplies that multiple Sole Hope teams had brought with them when they arrived. The boxes were mixed up and they needed to be sorted. Some were full of band-aids and gauze, others were full of shoe patterns for the tailors to sew together. After a couple hours of repacking supplies, we took a break and had lunch. Then Amber and I went to meet Dru and Asher who were playing with the kids.

"Hey guys!" Dru said when he saw us coming.

"Hi!" Amber said, "Chrissy, this is Dru, and that's Asher." I shook hands with Dru and Asher waved at me as she looked up from the kids she was playing with.

"Nice to meet you," Dru said in reply, "I'm guessing you've heard about what we're doing?"

"I have. My brother, Carter, and I are really close. He's told me a lot about it. Everything you guys are doing seems amazing."

"Thanks. It's been really great so far. Come meet the rest of the team," He added, motioning to all the women of various ages playing with kids. He introduced me to their three kids, Quinn, Asa, and Silas. Then he briefly introduced me to Kristi, Faith Ann, Taylor, Stacey and Jessica, the other team that was there serving. Trying to match names with faces, I continued playing with the kids while I exchanged small talk with Faith Ann and Stacey. Those children were absolutely precious, they were so glad we were there.

That evening we headed home for dinner and Amber cooked up a stir-fry with chicken, peppers and other vegetables. While eating, Amber said, "I think Friday we will start the clinics, there are still a couple things we need to work out before we can begin."

"Sounds good," I said in reply, and then rubbed my eyes.

"Are you tired yet?" Rob asked me laughing.

"Yeah, definitely."

"The time change is probably catching up with you, and you've been working all day. Why don't you head up to your room and get some sleep?"

"I will, thanks," I said, taking my plate to the sink and walking up to my room. I immediately changed into pj shorts and a t-shirt and crawled into bed. As my eyes closed and I started to drift off into unconsciousness, I could see the lights, and hear the music of Broadway in New York. I knew that I was doing the right thing by being in Uganda, but it was so hard to get the thought of New York and all of my friends out of my mind.

Chapter 12

The scorching, unrelenting sun caused sweat to roll down on my back in beads as we attempted to teach the giant swarm of children how to play freeze tag. Some of the children were carefree and simply played with each other, but some stood off by themselves with a look of confusion and loneliness on their faces. The pure expression on their faces, the look of longing and uncertainty was so different from the other children. Something about their countenance drew me to them and I did my best to love on them.

I was pushing a few of these children on the swings when I saw a nanny come in the orphanage through the big blue gate. She was carrying a little girl who looked to be about a year old.

"I'll be right back," I said to Amber, who was standing next to me. As the nanny took her down the steps to the main building, I followed her to the room she would stay in.

"You want to help?" the nanny asked me in choppy English.

"Yes," I said with a smile, grabbing the little gown and make-do cloth diaper from her hand, "What's her name?"

"Doesn't have name yet. We name her."

Almost instantly the name Ava popped into my head, it seemed perfect.

"What about Ava?" I suggested, pulling the gown over her tight, dark curls.

"I like that, her name is Ava," the nanny replied. I smiled as I picked her up off of the bed. "Where did you find her?" I asked.

"Police brought her. Found her at school."

"Maybe her parents were coming back for her."

"No. She abandoned."

My heart sank thinking that this little girl may have had no one to care for her, no Mom, no Dad, no one. It was then I felt a specific calling in the back of my mind.

But you are here...for six weeks you are here, Chrissy.

Little Ava had no one...except for me. I could care for her and love her as long as I was there. I decided at that moment that I would love Ava as much as I could, and hopefully earn the trust of the little girl who stared into my blue eyes with fear.

I was starting to believe what Carter had said: one life is all it takes to make a difference.

After a long night's rest we headed back to the orphanage Friday morning. I was secretly hoping that I would get to spend the day holding Ava; my heart was aching to see her. I walked past the room of highchairs where the babies ate and right away her chestnut eyes met mine. My mouth formed into a smile and I waved at her. Hesitantly she waved back. I finally took my eyes away from hers, knowing we had other things to do. When Amber and I walked into the storage room, we found all of the supplies had been sorted and prepared for the clinics.

"Today is the day," Paige said with a smile, walking in, "People will be getting here around nine o'clock for the first clinic. Dru, Asher and the whole Sole Hope team have been here for thirty minutes setting everything up. Each family who comes will need to be seated either on a stool for us to work on their feet, or on a bench to wait. They will have their feet cleaned, examined and then if we need to, we will take the jiggers out of their feet. After that they will get shoes and be on their way."

Wait, am I supposed to remember all of this? How do I even remove jiggers? No one has taught me these things!

"All right, sounds good. What time is it now?" I asked with a sense of false confidence.

"Eight fifty-eight, and there comes a family now!" A family trudged in the doors of the orphanage and a feeling of desperation came upon me. Their clothes were tattered and they were dirty. Despite their ragged

133

appearance they looked hopeful. As each member of the family came closer I noticed their feet. They were torn apart. I was surprised they were even able to make the walk to the orphanage. Asher then said something in Lugandan and told us to get them seated and begin washing their feet.

We guided them to where they would sit while other families were coming in the door. Paige sent them our way. I took a pair of rubber gloves from the bucket of supplies and snapped them on my hands. They had told me to sit and wash feet- I had a bucket of water, a bar of soap and a square of cloth to use as a washcloth. I rubbed the soap onto the washcloth and began running it over the dusty, tattered soles of a little boy's feet, only hoping my hands were gentle enough not to hurt his already injured toes.

Over the next several hours, many people sat in front of me. At first, the smell of dirty feet and rotting flesh was overwhelming but it seemed to lose its effect after a while. After their feet were cleaned someone else would then carefully removed the jiggers by digging into the soles of their feet and pulling them out. They would put the jiggers into a bucket and later they would all be burned. A third person would record on each person's record where the jigger had been so that when they came for a check-up, we could see how they were progressing. When we finished bandaging their feet they smiled and said, "Thank you," in Lugandan.

To them those couple of minutes of us working on their feet was life, it was healing. That afternoon, we were too busy to play with the kids because there were so many families to serve. They just kept coming, and coming and coming through the orphanage doors. I hoped that Monday when we came back to the orphanage, Ava would be waiting for me, maybe trusting me a bit more than she did the day before. I hoped that somehow she would see that she wouldn't be in that orphanage forever. For the first time since I had landed on Ugandan soil, I said a quick prayer. A prayer that one day she would have a family to call her own.

~~~~~~~~

Saturday, June 16th

I met the most precious baby girl Thursday. Well, she's really not a baby, she looks about a year and a half old. I even got to name her. She was being brought in and I went to help the nanny get her dressed. She told me she didn't have a name, so I suggested one and she liked it. Her name is Ava. She has tight black curly hair, much different than the other little girl's here and deep brown eyes that could melt your heart.

After writing about Ava, still dressed in my pajamas, I headed downstairs to find Rob and Amber eating breakfast.

135

"Good morning, Chrissy," Rob said.

"Morning. Sorry I'm late getting down here, I slept in a little bit."

"It's fine, we were going to take the day off anyway. Show you around a bit," Amber said.

My heart dropped when I realized I wouldn't be able to see Ava that day. Though a day off would be nice, I really wanted to see her.

"That would be great," I said, trying not to show my disappointment.

After eating some breakfast, I went upstairs to take a shower and get dressed. When I had finished, I walked downstairs and found Rob and Amber packing a bag with snacks. Together we loaded into the van and headed off to see the sights. We passed the blue gates of the orphanage with its creaky door barely hanging on to the hinges. Then we passed some shops. Shops that most people in America wouldn't dare to enter. One of the signs read: *Chicken, Ice Cream, Sausage.* What a combination. The doors to the shop were standing wide open, letting in not only fresh air but flies, gnats and mosquitos that would proceed to attack the mounds of fresh fruit.

Women were walking on the streets with babies tied onto their backs and baskets on their heads. *I would break my back doing that,* I thought as they did it with graceful ease. We passed what they would call houses and what I would call huts. They were made out of mud and sticks with tin roofs balanced on top. They were about the size of my bedroom back in the States. Most of the huts had goats and gardens with several banana trees out front.

"Is that one house?" I asked.

"Well, see that there are two buildings on one property?" Amber asked, pointing to a small area. Yes, there were two huts. One a little bigger than the other.

I nodded.

"They cook in one and sleep in the other. But yes, everyone sleeps in one of those little rooms."

"How many people?"

"Normally between six and eight"

Eight people in that room? No way. I couldn't imagine it.

As we continued on, we found men and women standing on the side of the roads trying to sell random items to people passing by. We drove out of town onto a bumpy dirt road with potholes everywhere. Suddenly Rob turned onto a narrow road with even tinier homes. Though the clothes the people wore were torn, they were as clean as they could possibly get them. It was evident that they took pride in the very few things they could call their own. Kids that were five and six years old were carrying their baby brothers and sisters on their backs, trying to bring water back to their families from miles away. Somehow, despite their circumstances, they were still smiling, proof of the joy inside.

As we continued on, we made our way by a sea of huts, another group of people. But this wasn't like the others. You could sense the desperation...the hopelessness. The smell alone was overwhelming. The people were filthy and the air was sticky. With no space in between each shack, it took me a moment to realize that this was where people actually lived.

"This is the one of the worst areas of Uganda. It is truly devastating, I want to take you here one day while you're here. I think the Sole Hope folks are talking about doing a clinic out here. Some of these people would not come all the way to the orphanage, it's such a far walk for them. People refer to this area of Uganda as the Masese slums. As you can see, they're very poor, and they have to walk miles to get somewhat clean water. There are over one million people in one square mile," Amber told me.

I was speechless, I had never in my life seen anything like this. The children on the side of the dirt paths looked up at me desperately, that joy we had seen in the faces of the other children was nowhere to be seen. These children were longing for love, longing for a different life than this one.

A little boy stood on the side of the road. He couldn't have been older than six. The infant in his arms was wailing despite his efforts to calm the screaming child. His eyes met mine and I just looked at him as we drove slowly away. I looked at him and wondered how things had ever come to this.

"Are you okay, Chrissy?" Amber asked.

"Yeah, I'm fine," was all that I could say. It was heartbreaking.

Chapter 13

On the other side of the slums we were once again greeted by the mountainous green country side. The hills were carpeted with trees and exotic flowers. Farmers were tending to their fields but all I could think of were the faces of the children we had just passed.

Among the shacks and huts along the sides of the roads, we would occasionally pass a mansion with the most elegant gardens. Amber informed me that the people who lived in those houses were probably government officials. We drove the long yet beautiful ride back to the guest house in quiet.

Saturday, June 16th
Rob and Amber showed me around a bit today, we went to the slums. People shouldn't have to live like that. I can't even begin to describe their conditions...the smell and the hopelessness. They are beyond poor. Those children were longing for love. They were desperately longing for a different life than that one.

That was all I could write. My thoughts wouldn't come together, I couldn't even write about the good part of the trip, about the beauty we had passed. All I could see were the little children with their tattered clothes and their scratched up bare feet.

My computer beeped from across the room; Carter wanted to Skype.

"Hey Carter! How are you?" I said, accepting his chat, thankful to see his face once again.

"I'm good, how are things going there?"

"Really good. Yesterday we started the jigger removal clinics and I met this little girl at the orphanage on Thursday, her name is Ava. She's adorable."

"I bet she is, how did you like Paige?"

"She's really awesome."

"I figured you girls would get along."

"Yeah, we talked almost the entire flight over."

"I'm so glad."

"How are you doing?"

"Pretty good actually, but I have to come off of my pain meds Monday, so it's gonna be kinda rough."

"I bet. Can I talk to Mom?"

"Actually, she's still sleeping."

"This late?"

"Chrissy, it's only 9:00 and she doesn't have to work today. Remember the time change?"

"Oh, yeah. I completely forgot!"

"So, how are you really doing? Emotionally?" his mood changed. His genuine concern returned.

"I'm okay. Really, I am. I mean, it's hard here by myself. But it's been good so far, not as bad as I thought it would be," I smiled.

"Have you been spending any time in your Bible?"

"Um," normally this question would have made panic rise in my chest." Not really. We've just been so busy with all of the clinics and everything. I haven't really had time."

"Promise me you'll read this week, okay?"

I nodded.

"Well, I better let you go, I'm sure you're pretty tired."

"I am, we went drove around today, and it was way more tiring than I thought."

"It's definitely emotionally exhausting. Go enjoy dinner, all right?"

"I will! Thanks."

"Love you."

"Love you, I'm praying for you."

"Thanks, bye."

"Bye." With this I shut the computer and made my way downstairs for dinner.

Instead of New York, it was that little boy holding the baby that I saw on the side of the road earlier who captured my thoughts as I was finally able to drift off to sleep that night. The piercing sound of the baby's cry in my mind broke the evening stillness.

142

The next morning I got up early. For the first time since I had arrived, I felt refreshed after our day off. I hopped in the shower to get ready for church. My mind was all over the place. I thought about Carter and how Hunter and I hadn't talked in a while. I found myself thinking about college and what I might major in.

Why am I thinking about these things? This is supposed to be a day off. I don't need to worry about any of this right now.

I got out of the shower and got dressed listening to the sounds of the street below. People bustled back and forth as they did every morning, but there was something different about that Sunday morning. It seemed as if they were slowing down a bit, realizing that it was the day you were supposed to rest.

Amber and Rob were busy preparing several dishes for lunch later that afternoon. The pastor and his family were joining us for a late lunch. After grabbing a quick bite for breakfast, I ran up upstairs, skipping a step here and there hurrying to fix my hair and put on some make up for the first time that week. I walked in my room and plugged my hairdryer in, not even thinking to put in the convertor first. Bam! My hairdryer blew. *Well done, Chrissy.* I thought to myself. *Great, what am I going to do now? It would be way too embarrassing to tell Amber…I'll just pull my hair up.* After pulling my half-dried hair up into a sloppy bun, I ran back downstairs barely catching Rob and Amber leaving for church.

"Did you hear that loud boom?" Amber asked me.

I laughed under my breath, "Um, yeah. Wasn't that weird?"

Together we walked down the dirt streets to church. Upon arriving, Rob and Amber greeted those sitting around us, introducing me as "Carter's sister." Like clockwork, everybody moved to their seats and sat down until announcements were made and everyone stood to sing. It was a missionary church so the songs were sung in English. But when it came time for the sermon, two men approached the stage. The first spoke in English and the other translated into Lugandan for those from Uganda.

While he spoke my mind wandered, wondering what my own family was getting ready to do that Sunday. I wondered if they would be going to church or if they were staying home with Carter since he wasn't supposed to be out and about yet. I wondered if Nathan had come to visit that weekend, or if Carly had gone to visit his family. Then, I wondered about Ava, what she would be doing.

After the service was over, we walked home and I helped Rob and Amber serve lunch to Pastor Dan, his wife, Anne, and their three kids. Becca was nine, Samuel was four, and Claire was nine months old. Pastor Dan shared that they had moved to Uganda a few years after their oldest child Becca was born when they felt the Lord was calling them to start a church in Uganda. After lunch, Becca, Samuel and I played hide-

and-go-seek while all of the adults talked about the Sole Hope project going on at the orphanage and how the church could help out.

While playing with little Samuel, my thoughts were again turned back to Ava who was sitting at the orphanage all by herself, probably wondering where she was and what she was doing there. I found myself anxious to get back to the orphanage the next day to hold her close and assure her that the orphanage wouldn't be her home forever.

After getting dressed the next morning, I headed downstairs. I sat down at the table with Amber and enjoyed the eggs and toast she had made.

"I'm going to double check with Dru but I think tomorrow we are going to go to the slums and hold a clinic. That way you can see the kids today," Amber said, smiling.

"Sounds good," I replied. On our walk to the orphanage that morning, everything we passed now seemed like routine; the smell of fresh fruit from the various shops, the women with baskets on their heads, the children walking to school. Once we arrived, Paige immediately greeted us saying, "We've had people coming in all weekend asking when the mzungus would be back to clean their feet, so I know we'll be busy today."

"I've heard that word..." I whispered to Amber. "Mzungu?"

"Yeah, that one. What does it mean?"

"White person!"

I laughed remembering all the times I had heard it. Saturday driving by the villages people had pointed to the van yelling, "Mzungu! Mzungu!"

"Dru mentioned going to the slums tomorrow to do a clinic. Do you know anything about that?" Amber asked Paige.

"That's what he said this morning. I know it's a long walk for them, so that will be really awesome," Paige said, and then turned to me, "Chrissy, even if we're busy this afternoon, I'll make sure you have time to see the kids."

"That would be great."

"I've also been informed by some of the nannies that they have a couple adoptive families coming in the next couple of weeks. That's gonna be really cool, make sure ya'll are here for that!" With a smile on my face we walked back to the storage room to finish gathering supplies for that day's clinic while people trickled slowly in the doors.

"Hi there," I said, bending down to one of the children coming in with his family to get their feet cleaned and examined. He just smiled and did the only thing a six year old can do when embarrassed: hide behind his mother's torn skirt. I showed them where they would sit to wait for their turn and as I walked off the little boy ran back to hug me tightly around the legs. The dirt that had always bothered me before didn't affect the sudden rush of love I had for this little boy. I leaned down and hugged him as his mother called to him and he darted away.

Later that day when I went to see Ava she was standing by herself but when she saw me her eyes lit up; I knew she remembered me. I walked up to her, held out my arms, and she walked into them immediately, hugging me so tightly. I put her up on my hip and we walked outside to play with the rest of the children. Her head was resting on my shoulder as I pushed a little boy on the swing. No matter what we did the rest of the afternoon, her little hand held tightly onto mine. When the nanny called all of the children for dinner, I sat her down beside some other little girls on a bench and helped serve food. Amber soon came in and told me it was time to go.

I walked up to Ava and whispered, "I will be back soon to see you."

This little girl now held a special place in my heart. I wanted her to know I would be back; I wanted her to know there was someone who cared about her.

The next day I woke up really early, as in five-thirty early. My Bible stared me in the face from its place on the desk across the room.

Fine. I'll read a Psalm or something.

"The Lord is merciful and gracious,
slow to anger and abounding in steadfast love."

I was in the middle of reading Psalm 103 when I got a Skype invitation from Hunter. *Odd. He knows it's really early here.* I realized I wasn't as excited to talk to him.

"Hey," I said, seeing him on the screen. He was all dressed up and looked like he had just gotten home from going to dinner.

"Hey, how are you?" he said smiling.

"Alright, it's 5:45 in the morning here, but how are you?"

"Good, how was your day yesterday?"

"Great, we're going to the slums to do a clinic today, I'm actually kind of excited about it." My words sounded unfamiliar and strange coming out of my mouth. *Since when am I excited about working in the slums?*

"Okay," he seemed like I was boring him out of his mind.

"What did you do yesterday?" I tried to change the subject.

"Matt, Josh, Tiffany and I went to see a movie and then went to dinner." *Um, Tiffany? Maybe we aren't as close as before, but cheating on me? So not cool.*

"Tiffany?" I questioned him.

"She's Josh's sister, just wanted to tag along. It's nothing. I promise."

"Okay, I'm assuming your parents aren't doing any better."

148

"Nope, oh, gotta go." He looked out his bedroom door frantically, "Sorry."

"Bye. Love you." With that he hung up immediately. Just lovely. I couldn't help but find myself wondering why I was so discontented with him lately. Not only being discontented... but wondering why he had called in the first place. He knew it was early, there had to have been a reason he called.

Around 6:00am, I hopped in the shower so I could reflect on everything I had just read and prayed over and talk to God about life...ask him what in the world he was doing.

Maybe this whole praying thing isn't as bad as I imagined, I thought, rinsing the shampoo from my hair. *God, maybe I've been underestimating you...*

When I got out, I saw I had missed two Skype calls from my mom and that there was an email from her in my inbox.

Chrissy,

We've hit a bump in the road. Carter has had a really high fever for the past couple of days. It has been around 103 degrees and he's been really achy all over. We went back to the hospital today. They are running tests. Pray for the results to come back clear and free of infection. Skype me as soon as you can. We love you and are praying for you to stay safe.

-Mom, Dad, Carly and Carter

No, God, no! I thought. *What if something more serious is wrong? What could happen? God, please keep him safe.* Tears filled my eyes and I buried my head in my hands. All I wanted was to be back home. I immediately pressed call on Skype, waiting impatiently and hoping they would answer. After a few minutes no one answered so I emailed Mom back.

Mom,
I'm praying. Please keep me updated. Tell Carter I love him.
-Chrissy

Trying to ignore the sinking feeling in the pit of my stomach, I kept going. When I had changed, I headed downstairs to find Rob and Amber already in the kitchen. I didn't tell them he was back in the hospital. I didn't want them to worry.

Dru, Asher, and the rest of the Sole Hope team met us at the guest house that morning. After everyone was ready, we packed lunches and left, starting off on our long drive. Just like every other drive we took, my face was covered with the red dirt from the dust by the time we arrived, making it look like I had a horrible spray tan.

When we arrived at the slums, people saw a bunch of mzungus approaching and they came rushing to the van. The red dirt of the ground covered them and they already looked tired as they stood in the sweltering heat. Amber handed me some lollipops to give out to the children, and when I gave one to each of them their faces lit up. Their big brown eyes were filled with joy, and a smile of gratefulness formed on their faces. I scanned the massive crowd of people for that little boy. I knew it was virtually impossible to find him in the sea of faces but I looked anyway.

We began to set up the clinic and everyone watched with curious, wide eyes. All the stools were unloaded from the van and some of the villagers brought out benches from the nearby school. Each bucket was placed by a stool and filled with water and medicated soap. Off to the side, I sorted shoes as everyone ran around doing different things to get the clinic going.

The people still sat by contently and watched. Dru and Asher figured out which children needed to have their feet worked on. One by one they came and each sat at a stool to have their feet treated. Some of them were worse than others. An older man had over forty jiggers and a young boy had fifty. I watched in awe while the ladies used razor blades and safety pins to remove these parasites and only a few tears ran down their cheeks, if any. I bandaged their feet carefully and placed shoes lovingly on their soles.

Two hours into our day, a child was placed on the stool in front of me. I looked up and smiled at the little boy. My heart stopped. His eyes…it was him! The little boy from the other day.

"One life is all it takes." Carter's voice replayed in my mind once again.

Thank you, God. Out of all the children here, he is the one that gets placed in front of me. What a sweet gift.

I wrapped his feet with even greater care. They were torn to pieces, just like many of the others. With gloved hands, I rubbed cream onto his wounds, wrapping them with gauze. As I bandaged I prayed for healing.

We worked on the feet of sixty children before packing up the clinic that afternoon. The others would have to be done on a different day. Afterwards we were invited into the pastor's home. He was the one who had organized the clinic. Before heading back to the guest house he guided us around the village. Though his home was a bit larger, a bit nicer than the others the rest of the houses were more like little mud or stick huts. Just driving by from the road I didn't think it could look any worse than it did. Oh, was I wrong. As we walked, I was again aware of the smell. It seemed to grow with each step.

People crowded in the little shacks. Eight people into one room, sometimes more. While the interior of the ramshackle buildings didn't consist of much, the dirt floors were kept as clean as possible. Those who had pots and pans used the dirty water to wash them. Several families were preparing a meal for supper. Some had no food. There was nothing to prepare. The hunger that had arisen in my stomach throughout the day lessened knowing theirs was so much greater.

They deserve so much more than this, I thought, wishing there was something I could do.

On our way home, staring out the window at the beautiful surroundings, my thoughts were turned back to Carter. When he had gotten hurt, all I wanted was for him to be okay. Now that he was sick, I found myself wishing for that all over again. But I knew that he was safe, that he was being taken care of. Some of the people I had seen that day needed to be hospitalized; they needed more care than we could give them in a few short minutes. They needed so much more than medical healing.

Amber spoke, interrupting my thoughts, "Chrissy, shortly after we get back, another missionary couple, Cheryl and Stephen Moore, will be arriving. They have a son your age, James and a little girl, Ruthie, who is six. They are also missionaries in church planting."

"All right, how long will they be here?"

"They will stay with us at least through the summer, maybe longer. They'll be with us until they can find a place of their own. It will be a good transition for them since we are taking a break right now and working with Sole Hope."

"Wait, if their son is my age, how is he going to finish high school?"

"They have been on the mission field in Mozambique since James was very young, so he's been homeschooled."

"Oh, okay." The first thought that came to my mind was Hunter. I could only imagine his reaction when I told him there was a seventeen year old boy staying in the guest house with us.

By the time we reached the guest house, it was time for us to fix dinner for the Moores.

Chapter 14

"Hi, welcome to Uganda," Amber said answering the door to the Moores, hugging Cheryl as if they had been friends for years.

"Thank you. We are so glad to finally be here," Cheryl said, "This is James, Ruthie, and of course, my husband Stephen."

"It's very nice to meet you, I'm Amber."

"I'm Rob," he said introducing himself.

"And I'm Chrissy," I said, shaking hands with everyone.

"Very nice to meet you all," Stephen said.

"Well, Chrissy, would you and Rob show them around while I finish dinner?" Amber said.

"Of course."

"This is the guest bedroom," Rob said as we made our way across the living room to the bedroom door.

"Ruthie, James, you guys will stay in here," Stephen said.

"Sorry to cram you two together, I wish we had another bedroom for one of you," Rob commented as they put their bags down inside the door.

"That's okay, I really don't mind," James said, giving his sister's ponytail a tug with a smile, to which she responded by pushing him. He stood beside me and I noticed his hair, then his height, then his nicely cut jaw line, all which caught me off guard.

I wasn't expecting him to be so cute.

"So when did you all start considering the mission field?" Rob asked at dinner that night, after we had given them the 'grand tour. '

"Right after James had started kindergarten we felt like God was calling us to go, but since he had just started school it didn't make much sense," Cheryl said.

"But the thought kept coming to both of us so at the beginning of his first grade year we knew we had to follow God's calling. We moved to Mozambique through the same organization as you guys for church planting ten years ago when James was seven," Stephen said, continuing Cheryl's story.

"I was born there!" Ruthie said with her little voice.

"Yes, you were, honey," Cheryl said, "And then a few months ago we received an email that was sent out to several missionaries telling them of the need for church planters in specific parts of Uganda. We already had four couples in Mozambique working on church planting and a couple of dozen churches grounded, so we felt like we had done what we could do in that area of Mozambique and that God was calling us here."

"Now we're here until God calls us somewhere else," James concluded their story.

"That's awesome. My brother Carter is twenty-four, and he is a journeyman, working with Rob and Amber," I said.

"Where is he?" James asked me.

"Well, it's a long story."

"We have all night," he said as Rob and Amber started to clean up.

"He actually works here, but he came home for a month break about six weeks ago. He was scheduled to come back almost two weeks ago."

"What happened?" James asked curiously.

"We were on our way to breakfast and, well, I was driving and another car hit us on the passenger side," I was at a loss for words, realizing this was only the second time telling someone, "He broke his right leg and his right foot."

"Wow. So, you're here in his place?" His eyes were full of compassion, reminding me of the way Carter's looked when we were deep in conversation.

I nodded, it was starting to feel a bit awkward since everyone else had moved to the living room. I was a bit surprised by him, he was so interested in my story, genuinely interested in what God was doing in my life.

"But I really didn't want to come," I said.

"Why?" He gave me a questioning glance.

"I had to miss a trip to New York to get here."

"Oh."

"Yeah. How did you feel when your parents told you that your family would be going to the mission field?"

"Since I was so young I didn't want to leave my home or my friends and didn't understand why we were moving, it just didn't make any sense to me."

"Understandable."

"I really couldn't help it; I was only seven when we moved, but once we got there I ended up loving it. By the time I was fourteen I definitely knew that God had us in Mozambique for a reason and that it had always been His plan."

"That's big faith."

"It makes me think of Hebrews eleven. God did all of those things by faith. I'm so thankful my parents moved in faith when I was so young and moved us to the mission field."

He is a dream. What teenage boy talks like that? Wow. His jawline is the definition of perfection.

I came out of my trance, "Are you nervous coming here from Mozambique?"

"Sort of, I kind of know what to expect though. It was hard to leave everyone in Mozambique, all of my friends are there. We had been living around most of them for years."

"Well I can tell you that the orphanage and the slums have opened my eyes to so much. It helps that all of those kids are so cute."

"In the last couple of years I loved being able to go to the orphanage with Ruthie and volunteer. We got to see so many kids adopted, it was incredible."

"That's amazing. How often do you guys go back to the States?"

"We stay here anywhere from three to four years. When we come home, it's between a three to six month furlough. We just got back from furlough two months ago so we won't go back for another couple of years."

"Is it weird, going back to the States after being here for such a long time?"

"It really is, I like it here much better. But it's all I've ever known for the last ten years."

"James," Cheryl yelled, "You two come here for a second."

"Be right there," he responded." We're being summoned," he turned to me.

"Yes, Mom," James said walking into the living room where everyone else was.

"I was just wondering what ya'll were doing."

"Just talking," He responded, looking down at me for a few seconds. It was then I noticed his eyes were a blue…a stunning bright blue, and I couldn't take *my* eyes off of them.

"Yeah, just talking," I said, pulling my eyes away from his gaze, and turning to Amber, "We should play a card game."

"What game?" Amber said.

"Hyjack, it's really fun. My sister taught me how to play."

"All right, let's play," Stephen said.

By the end of the game I had come to love the Moore family, they were so much fun. Our time together that night reminded me of the nights spent together as a family before Carter left for Uganda. The time spent together as a family laughing, playing games and watching movies flooded my mind as we played an intense game of hyjack.

We finished our game and I excused myself to my room to try and Skype Carly. After meeting James and talking with him…getting a small glimpse into his heart, I had to talk to her.

"Chrissy!" She exclaimed when she answered.

"Hey!" She looked exhausted.

"How's it going?"

"With the exception of Carter being sick, great. How is he? I've been a nervous wreck since I got Mom's email."

"He's okay, we're still at the hospital waiting for test results. These people take forever."

"Well, they have other patients."

"True."

"Do they have him on any kind of medicine to keep the fever down?"

"He's been on an antibiotic since his surgery but it's not bringing the fever down as much as they would like.

Now, how's your trip?" Carly's mood lightened as she changed the subject.

"Actually, it's been really good. I met this sweet baby girl and even got to name her, and today a new missionary family got here."

"Carter told us about the little girl. Ava, right?"

"Yeah, anyway, I wanted to talk you to about something."

"Okay."

"This missionary family that got here today? They have a son my age. His name is James."

"I can see where this is going."

I rolled my eyes and continued, "Okay, just picture the cutest guy ever. Blue eyes, *really* blue eyes, nice brown hair, and he's tall."

"So, like Nathan?" She smiled.

I laughed, "And he loves Jesus so much. I could tell by just the one conversation we had."

"Chrissy? You're forgetting something. You have a boyfriend."

"I know," I sighed, "That's my problem."

"Well, just remember, you didn't go to Uganda to get a new boyfriend."

"I know."

"Just keep that in mind."

"Well, Mom and I are getting ready to go back to the hospital," she said, glancing at her phone screen.

"Okay, love you. Tell everybody I said hi."

"Will do. Love you too!" With this we hung up and I pulled out my journal, I knew I needed to get my thoughts off of boys, especially since Carter wanted me to be focusing on God. But nothing could take the new found smile off of my face.

Tuesday, June 19th

Today we went to the slums to do a clinic, it was heartbreaking. Their situations are so sad. Devastating actually. But it was amazing to see how happy they were when they left with bandaged feet. Just a few minutes working on their feet but it meant so much to them. OH! And the other day I saw this little boy-six maybe- holding his little brother or sister who was screaming. Out of all those kids he was seated in front of me so I could bandage his feet. So very amazing.

Yesterday I got to see Ava again. She is just precious. And a new family came today, Cheryl and Stephen Moore. They have a son my age, named James and a daughter named Ruthie who is five. And to add to the craziness that is my life- back at home Carter is back at the hospital. He has a really high fever. They are running tests. I'm so worried. I haven't told anyone yet. The end. I'm done. And exhausted.

P.S. I know this isn't important...but James has STUNNING blue eyes.

Chapter 15

"There you are," James said. Ava and I were outside playing on the swings while Amber helped tidy everything up from the clinic the previous day.

"Were you looking for me?" I turned to see him walking up behind me.

"Not really. So you've made a friend, I see."

A pang of disappointment hit my chest. *I was kind of hoping he was looking for me.*

"Yep, I met her last Thursday. Her name is Ava. Isn't she adorable?" I stopped her swing and stepped around to look at her.

"Very," he agreed, starting to tickle and smile at her.

"When do you go back?" he asked me, changing the subject abruptly.

"July 16th. But right now, I've got to feed dinner to a bunch of cute kids." I lifted Ava from her swing and carried her with me inside.

"Can I join you?" he asked, walking with the two of us.

"If you want to," I said, trying not to smile too much.
*I can't start to like him. I can't start to like him.
Even though he loves Jesus a whole whole lot and has
blue eyes that could melt any girls heart-not to mention a
killer smile- I cannot start to like him.*

When we got back from the orphanage that night, I
had another email from my mom. My heart was
pounding as I opened it.

Chrissy,

We're still waiting for results, it's been almost two
days, should get results sometime today or tomorrow.
His fever has gone down some, but not significantly.
Keep praying.

-Mom

I took a deep breath and went downstairs to help
Amber start preparing supper. Several of the ladies who
were working with Sole Hope at the orphanage were
coming over to the house for dinner.

"You've been here for two weeks now and somehow
I don't really know a whole lot about you. All I know is
that your brother adores you and talks about you all the
time," Amber said out of the blue.

"Well, I'm seventeen and I'll be a senior next year," I
replied, not really knowing what to say. Her statement
had caught me off guard.

"Have you been thinking about college?"
The college question, really?

"A little, my mom really wants me to go to Gardner-Webb like my sister."

"Do you? How old is your sister?"

"I already know my way around there, so I'm definitely thinking about it. And Carly is twenty-one. She'll be a senior this year."

"It's a very good school, that's where I went. I really matured a lot in my faith there, too. At your age, it's so important to be rooted to a group of believers that will hold you accountable."

"Carter always tells me that, so does Carly. When Carter left for college, things were so different at home," I said, not realizing how open I was being with her. The peppers we were chopping smelled sweet, the onions- *not so much. If I start to tear up for some reason*, I thought, *I can blame it on the onions.*

"What do you mean?"

"I mean, he was always the one who made sure I was at church and in Bible study. He made sure that I was reading my Bible daily. Then when he left I didn't have him to keep me accountable." After the multiple conversations with Carly and Carter these facts rolled off of my tongue like no big deal.

"That makes a lot of sense. I bet it was really hard when he left, wasn't it?" Her voice was full of compassion.

"Yeah, I was only twelve when he left for college, and then I was sixteen when he left last year to come here. Knowing he was in Uganda was so hard. When he

165

was away at college I knew I could call him and we could talk, but in Uganda it's not like that. I couldn't go to him and tell him I was struggling, ask him how to help my boyfriend whose parents were struggling with their marriage."

"I know how you feel, I had a sister who was four years older than me who left for college, quickly got married after graduating and moved to Georgia with her husband. That was really hard for me." She paused, looked thoughtful for a bit and then seemed to rush forward, "I had a boyfriend when I was your age, too. I wish I wouldn't have done that."

"Why?" Great, now she was bringing up the boyfriend thing, looking back I cannot believe I was so open with someone I had known for such a short time.

"He wasn't a very godly young man. My friends begged us to go on a date, so we did, just so they would leave us alone. He ended up cheating on me after a year. I wish now that I would have saved my heart for Rob, saved my heart for the right man."

"Yeah. Hunter and I go to school together and we were in a bunch of the same classes. His friends started hanging out with my friends and we went to dinner and few weeks later we began dating. He used to go to church every week, so did we." *How much should I tell her?*

"Then his parents started fighting and he stopped going. That was about a month after we started dating."

Amber continued, "I know looking back that I wish I wouldn't have dated the guys I went out with in high school. I'm sure I grew from those relationships but I wish I hadn't given my heart away to so many different boys. Not all of them were bad guys, I just wish I had saved my heart for my future husband." She stopped and pulled a few boxes out of the pantry, "I know it's hard, but you have to stay focused on what God has in store for your life and the plan he has for you," she said looking right in to my eyes, "You just have to learn to follow him."

"Sometimes it's just so hard to see what he is doing," I confessed.

"It really is. I know when your brother got in the car wreck, you had to be questioning God. Rob and I were also. We didn't know why he had to get hurt right when we were about to start with Sole Hope, but we've discussed that now we do."

"You do?"

"Yes. It's because God had another plan for all of us. I know it must have seemed unfair that God allowed your brother to be hurt to bring you here, and that your boyfriend's parents are fighting. I know it's easy to focus and think about what *you* can do to make your life better, but the best thing to do is to pray and ask God for guidance in what decisions to make. Maybe it is your friends or your boyfriend or stress at school, but whatever it is, ask God continually what to do. He will give you an answer. Whether or not it's what you were hoping for, it's His plan for your life. He will be faithful to give you wisdom."

"It's just hard sometimes, to know that God *is* doing the best thing in my life," I actually started to tear up.

"It really is, but all I can tell you is that you have to pray and ask Him for answers. I remember when I felt God calling Rob and me to Uganda, I had to approach Rob and we prayed about it. At first we didn't want to come here at all, it just didn't seem to make sense to us. I mean, we had just gotten married and were really involved with our small group back home. Slowly our hearts were changed and we knew it was His plan for us."

"When Carter told me he wanted me to come here, I thought he was crazy. I gave up a trip to New York to come in his place." For the first time at the sound of the words *New York* I didn't feel jealousy. I didn't feel a pull to be there with the rest of my class.

"Really? He didn't tell us that."

"Yep. It was a hard decision to make. In the end, I came solely because Carter needed me to, not because I felt like it was the right thing to do." Embarrassment turned my cheeks pink. For the first time I felt guilty at this confession. I worried she would be judging me for not wanting to come serve.

"I bet it was," she looked at her watch, and washed her hands, "Well, I better head upstairs and shower off before Paige and Anne Marie get here."

Relief flooded my being, there was no judgment in her expression whatsoever.

"All right," I said, washing my hands, "I probably will too," and then we both walked up the stairs. When we got to her bedroom door I said, "Thanks Amber."

"You're welcome, any time Chrissy," she said making her way into the bedroom. I sat on the edge of my bed and began to pray, awkwardly at first, not really knowing what to say, "Lord, help me to remember all that Amber and I have talked about. Show me how to make the changes in my life that need to be made and help me to make them with your wisdom and guidance. I pray you would show me your will in all situations in my life. And it would be really awesome if you could heal Carter completely. God, I'm so worried about him. In Your name, Amen."

Chapter 16

The whole night while Paige and Anne Marie were there, I could think of nothing but the conversation Amber and I had earlier. That and the fact that Carter was back in the hospital. When they had left later that night, I headed up to my room, sat down on the side of my bed and picked up my Bible. Flipping through the pages, I came to Psalms and a note fell out of my Bible and onto the floor.

Chrissy,

I really hope you read this before you come home. I'm praying for you every day.

When I was in Uganda for the first time, I found myself thinking about a lot of things that I was struggling with. The passages I found comforting were 1 Peter 5:6-7, Psalm 55:22, Romans 8:28, and lastly, Jeremiah 29:11. I hope you'll take a minute and read through them. I love you.

Love, Carter

Smiling, I turned to 1 Peter 5:6-7, "Humble yourselves, therefore, under God's mighty hand, that he may lift you up in due time. Cast all your anxiety on him because he cares for you."

Because He cares for you.

Then I turned to Psalm 55:22, "Cast your cares on the LORD and He will sustain you; He will never let the righteous be shaken."

He will sustain you.

I flipped to the next passage, Romans 8:28, "And we know that for those who love God all things work together for good, for those who are called according to His purpose."

Work together for good.

Lastly, I came to a verse I had memorized when I was in Kindergarten at church...the verse I still remembered by heart, "For I know the plans I have for you declares the Lord, plans to prosper you and not to harm you. Plans to give you a hope and a future."

While reading this verse, I found tears rolling down my cheeks and onto the pages of my Bible, blurring several words. I took one finger and tried to wipe them off the pages, but didn't bother to wipe them off of my face.

When I read this, I knew that God had ordained this moment. I knew that He had planned to use Carter's words to further work in my heart. I grabbed my laptop and opened up my email, sending a quick note to Carter.

"I just wanted to let you know I found that note in my Bible. I read it, and I know God led me find it at just the right time. Just like you, I have a lot on my mind, and things are laying heavily on my heart. I'm trying to make the smartest and most godly decisions for my life. So, thanks. Love you and can't wait to see you. I'm actually having an incredible time but you remain forefront in my thoughts and I am praying for you all the time…praying that God will protect you. - Chrissy"

After I sent the email I crawled into bed. My face still wet with tears, I realized I was at peace. I hadn't noticed before that moment how discontented I must have been. I felt like I could breathe easier than I had in a long time.

Wednesday, June 20th

Amber and I just talked about life…and boys…and what in the world God is trying to do. The puzzle is starting to come together. And I can't believe I haven't seen it all this time. God has been trying to talk to me for so long, but I just stood there ignoring Him. And finally I'm beginning to hear Him, what He's saying exactly- I have no idea. But I know it's more than I expected.

Tears cascaded onto the pages of my journal as I felt God moving into my heart. I could feel Him in me, using me to write these words and process these thoughts that I never would have expected to come from me.

The next day, I woke up ready to face whatever the day would bring.

"You don't happen to play soccer, do you?" James asked me, during lunch that day.

He plays soccer, too?!?

"I have a little bit of experience, why?" I shot back playfully at him.

I haven't played since fourth grade but yes, I play soccer! I'll go practice right now if you're asking me to play.

"There's a group of little boys who are dying to play, but I can't be on my own team. Want to join me at the field across the street?"

"After lunch," I said, grinning.

"Cool," he said taking a bag full of cotton balls and band-aids to a foot washer, flashing me a killer smile while walking away.

"You're good," James said during a short break in our game thirty minutes later.

My calves were burning and I couldn't catch my breath.

Those kids are fast! I haven't gotten that much exercise in...a long time.

"Thanks," I said coolly, trying to hide the fact that my legs hurt so bad I didn't know if I could take another step." Not bad yourself. I played with our church kindergarten through fourth grade. After that I wasn't interested."

"The kids in Mozambique taught me everything I know, they're way better than me, even after years of playing with them."

Truth was, he was better than Carter who had played all the way through high school. Those kids from Mozambique had taught him well.

"These kids are pretty good too." I glanced at him, then back at our make-do field.

"It's amazing how much better kids are here than back at the states when it comes to sports like this. When you don't have a TV or video games to distract you, you're able to get really good at what you love. For these kids it's soccer."

"That's true," I said, as the kids started pulling us back onto the field." Apparently our break is over,"

"We can try our best but neither of us can beat them. Quite impressive for four and five year olds," he said grinning.

That night after dinner I got a quick shower and sat down to read an email from my mom. Once again, my heart was pounding, but before I could read anything I saw the Skype icon flashing at me from the corner of the screen.

"Hey Mom," I said, I could see both my mom and Dad on the screen with worried expressions.

"Chrissy, the doctors were right. It is more than just a fever. He has what's called bacteremia," She said hesitantly.

"What is that?" Tears welled in my eyes quickly and my throat began to burn.

"It's a staph infection that enters your bloodstream. We know that it is very serious. He more than likely got it after the surgery on his foot. It affects your bones and muscles and if it makes it all the way up his body it could affect his heart and lungs. However, the doctor said that because we caught it relatively early it probably won't make it all the way up to his heart. Nevertheless..." She began to cry and Dad picked up for her.

"We need to keep praying. Praying it won't travel very far. They started pumping penicillin in his IV to prevent the infection from spreading."

I nodded as tears fell down my cheeks.

"We think you should stay," he said, "Carter told us he wants you to stay. He says he knows God is going to do mighty things. It's all going to be fine."

"Okay," tears ran rapidly down my face.

"Can you tell Rob and Amber for us?"

"Yeah."

"We love you, honey."

"I love you too," I managed through tears.

"Just pray, hard," he said.

"I will," I said, wiping at my cheeks.

"You better get to bed, okay?"

"Okay. Keep me posted."

"We will. Love you, sweetie," my mom said.

"Love you too. Bye."

"Bye," they said hanging up. I buried my head in my hands and sobbed. *God you have to heal him!* I cried. *You can't let him die! I can't lose him. Not now. I just don't understand. I was just starting to feel you move- why now? I don't understand!*

Ten minutes later I heard a knock at the door.

"Come in," I said, wiping the last of the tears from my face.

"Hey, it's me, you all right?" Amber said, peeking her head into the door.

"Yeah. Just missing home." I didn't know how to tell her about Carter, about how sick he really was. The guilt piled up...

I took this time from Carter. If we wouldn't have gotten in that stupid car wreck, he would have been here. He would have been healthy...

"Can we talk?"

"Sure," I replied nervously, not knowing what she would say next.

"I just wanted to tell you how proud I have been of you so far. It's not easy to be gone from your family for so long. You have done so well, Chrissy."

"Thanks, it's been hard, but I'm really thankful God opened up the door for me to come."

"We have enjoyed having you so much," Amber said kindly.

176

I smiled weakly.

"You sure you're okay? You seem kind of out of it tonight."

"Actually, there's something I need to tell you," I paused to take a deep breath, trying to prevent the tears. She nodded me on.

"Carter is sick, really sick. A couple days ago my parents emailed me and told me that they had to take Carter back to the hospital because he was aching all over and he had a fever of 103 for several days," the words poured out faster than I had intended them to, "They skyped me tonight…" Tears fell from my eyes, "He has a staph infection in his blood stream, I don't remember what it's called, a big word that starts with a 'b.' But they know it's serious. His doctor said that because they caught it so early they should be able to get rid of it before it spreads to his heart and lungs."

Her eyes went wide." Oh, Chrissy. Why didn't you tell me before?"

"I didn't want you to worry," there were tear drops all over my pants.

"You should have told me. This is way too much for you to handle by yourself."

"I'm sorry. I just…" She wrapped me in her arms and I held onto her tightly as we sat on my bed while I cried and cried and cried.

"I'm so scared, Amber."

"I know."

"I could finally feel God moving, and now…"

"I don't understand either." I pulled out of our hug.

"They said I should stay," I stammered as I blew my nose into some tissue she had gotten for me from the bathroom.

"Okay, do you want to?"

"Yeah, Carter wants me to."

"Then I think you should."

"Me too."

"All right, that's enough of that," Amber wiped a tear from her own eye, "Let's talk about how I saw you and James looking at each other today."

I laughed." It's noticeable?"

"Very!"

That reminded me…I needed to talk to her about Hunter." This may seem weird, but the whole boyfriend thing, what should I do? When we first started dating we went to church together weekly. That only lasted a couple months. His parents starting fighting and it was like he became a totally different person. His walk with God had seemed so evident in the beginning and it just keeps fading and fading.

"Maybe it's that this whole time he's just been putting up an act, like his entire walk with God was just a front. I mean, maybe that's how I was, too and we were both doing it together so it didn't seem like a big deal," the words coming out of my mouth were new to me. I had only thought these things over briefly. But coming out of my mouth they sounded so different…" so realistic.

178

"You've been thinking about this a lot?" Amber gave me a smile.

"I guess I have."

"Well," she sat down on the bed beside of me." When I was just about your age I went to summer camp with my church. There was this one guy in our youth group who I'd had a crush on for years. We had just started dating a couple weeks before camp. While at camp, I got really close to the Lord. He just moved in my life and did things in my heart that I will never forget. When we got home, this guy didn't understand the change that had happened in me while we were gone and of course he was the same guy as before.

"Looking back I see how foolish I was to keep dating him but I was young and didn't know what I was doing. After a year, I continued to grow in the Lord and he was still lukewarm in his faith. I knew it wasn't going to work anymore so I broke up with him. But it's not as easy as it sounds, I know."

"I do feel like I need to break up with him," *did I just say that?* "But like you said, it's hard. Lately it feels like all he cares about is what's wrong in his world and he doesn't want to spend time with me, much less God. My perspective on all of this has changed so much. I know that he needs to be in a right relationship with God and loving Him above all else before ever having a relationship with me. And that's not happening."

"Chrissy, you have a really good take on all of this. You're right, God needs to be first, then his family, then you. He needs to constantly show that he loves God and that he cares for you. At this age, boys are still trying to grasp girls and dating, too, just like most girls are. But of course, as everyone knows, boys take longer than girls to mature." We both laughed and broke the tension as she continued, "My advice for you would be for you to go to the Word and pray for guidance and wisdom. You said his parents are struggling, right?"

"Yeah. They're getting a divorce. I don't want to disappoint him, I feel like I should still be there for him."

"You can still be there for him. If he's honoring you, but not God, it's definitely something to think about. I know it's hard for you to make this choice and it makes it even harder because you want to be there for him while he's going through this tough situation."

"It really is, and you're right."

"You need to be praying for his parents, and for him. Most of all you need to trust God to give you direction and guidance in this situation. Even if it's not the answer you want, He will give you the answer. That's the biggest lesson I have ever learned. You need to trust God no matter what the situation is."

"Thanks Amber, I really just needed someone that I could talk to, that would understand what I'm going through."

"Absolutely." She paused, "Can I pray over you? For guidance and for Carter."

This didn't make me as uneasy as I thought it would have. "Sure."

"Lord," she began to pray as she covered my hands with hers, "I just thank you so much for the gift you have given to me in Chrissy. She has come at just the right time to be such a help to Rob and to me. God, you have been moving so mightily in her heart. You have lit a new spark in her life that I don't ever think will go out. Lord, I pray You would wrap your mighty arms around her in this difficult time. She is working through a lot of tough decisions in her life and I ask you would give her your wisdom and your knowledge in what is best for her life. Father, we need You to heal Carter." Her voice caught and she paused to gain composure, "Comfort Chrissy and her family. God, we pray again for protection for Carter, for healing, for a miracle, Lord. We know You can do anything and that Your will is going to be done no matter what. We know there is no power that can stand before You or stop you from doing mighty things. Lord, we love You. Thank You for all you are doing and all that you will do."

We sat and hugged for a few more minutes and I cried some more. She finally stood up and we hugged before she left, "Seriously Chrissy, I'm here whenever you need me. Even if it's three in the morning, I don't care."

"Okay."

"If you get the chance, listen to the song, *Great I Am.* It's amazing. I have a feeling it would be a huge comfort to you. It's helped me through some of my hardest moments in life."

"Thanks." She walked out and I curled up in my bed. My tears were dried; it seemed as if suddenly they had all run out. There was no time to think through what had just happened, I fell fast asleep in a matter of minutes.

I woke up suddenly, rolling over in bed expecting to see that only thirty minutes had passed. To my own surprise I found that I had been asleep for over five hours. I could see the Skype icon flashing across the room. Panic flooded my chest. *Oh no! Carter!*

I jumped out of bed and opened Skype.

"Hunter?" I whispered to myself as my nerves subsided.

What in the world? Really, God? Do I have to talk to him right now? I accepted his invite anyway. He had to know it was four in the morning, there had to be a reason he called.

"Hey Chrissy," he said looking at me with the look of exhaustion.

"Hunter."

"Yeah?"

"Carter is back in the hospital." Just the slightest amount of concern showed on his face.

"Oh really? What happened?"

"He has a staph infection in his bloodstream- it's really serious. If it spread to his heart and lungs…well, it could......"

"Oh."

"Yeah. Just pray, okay?" I was trying to be nice to him but my conversation with Amber kept playing over in my head. *Save your heart for the man you will marry one day.*

"Yeah," he nodded and his face read, *yeah, right, like that's going to happen.*

So, it's four in the morning. I was actually getting really good sleep for the first time in a really long time. Do you have something life changing to tell me or did you just want an early morning Skype with your girlfriend? I restrained all of these things and kindly said, "Anyway, how was your day?"

Four in the morning here, ten at night there.

"Pretty good, Tiffany, Josh and I hung out for a while and then Mom said we had to go to dinner as a family. Well, I guess by family, she means the two of us now but we just got home. I've got a lot going through my head. I just wanted to talk."

"Oh, okay." *Did he really just mention her again? Oh, whatever,* "Today was really good here, my trip has been so amazing, well aside from Carter being back in the hospital of course," I rubbed my forehead and then my heart began to race as I began to tell him everything that had been happening at the orphanage and with Sole Hope throughout the week." I met this precious little girl named Ava and when we went to the slums to do a clinic with Sole Hope we worked on over sixty children's feet. You wouldn't believe," I continued, he stopped me mid-sentence.

"Wow, I didn't know washing feet and playing with orphans was your new forte. Don't you have anything interesting to tell me about? I'm not trying to be mean, but your days must be really boring since you do the same thing day after day."

Oh. My. Word. Unbelievable! I'm serving others, and what is he doing? Cheating on me with someone two years younger than him.

"Hunter, I've got to go." *Got to go before I say anything I'll regret.*

"Oh, well, okay. Skype me later."

I nodded and pressed the escape button- *I think God just gave me His answer about Hunter. Maybe I am beginning to see things more clearly.*

Chapter 17

It was 6:15am by the time I rolled out of bed the next morning. My thoughts immediately turned to Carter. I desperately wanted to call and check in on him but I knew my family would be sound asleep. I downloaded the song Amber had suggested and then went downstairs to eat and found Amber at the kitchen table.

"Hey kiddo. Get any sleep last night? You're up pretty early," Amber said when I walked in.

"Actually, I got a solid five hours before getting a Skype call from the last person I wanted to talk to at four in the morning." I rolled my eyes and smiled, "You?"

She laughed, "Tossed and turned mostly but I'm sure I'll make up for it later."

After eating I made the trek upstairs to my room to read my Bible. Before I started reading I grabbed my phone and decided to go outside to spend time with God. I knew I wouldn't make it through the day without time in His Word. I sat down on the porch swing, opened my Bible to Psalm and began to read.

As I wrote in my journal, I had *Great I Am* repeating in my ears.

Friday, June 22nd

Carter has a staph infection in his blood stream. He's back in the hospital. I'm terrified, worried...scared. I just want him to be okay. I was just starting to hear God. Where is He now? Why can't He just fix it all? I'm just praying He will. Amber told me to listen to the song "Great I Am." It's amazing.

"The mountains shake before Him, the demons run and flee, at the mention of your name, King of Majesty. There is no power in hell, or any who can stand before the power and the presence of the Great I Am, The Great I Am..."

So comforting to know that even though He's not fixing it now... He's still in control of it all.

Tears were dripping slowly down my face again, blurring the words in my journal once more. Those words wouldn't have come out of my mouth two weeks ago. All of a sudden I heard the screen door open and slam shut.

"Oh, hey," James said, when he saw me sitting there.

"Hey," I said, as I tried to stop crying, and wiping the tears quickly off my face.

"What's the matter?" His face filled with concern so quickly.

"Oh, nothing."

"I know that's not true," he said laughing, "Really, what's wrong?" His voice was full of compassion as he sat down beside me.

"I found out last night that my brother, Carter, is back in the hospital."

"Why?" his voice was panicked.

"He had a high fever for several days and they took him back. They found out yesterday that he has a staph infection in his blood stream. It's really, really serious. If the infection spreads to his heart or lungs…" I couldn't finish I started crying so hard. To my surprise, I felt his arms wrapped around me tightly. I found myself resting my head on his shoulder feeling as if I was sitting beside Carter.

"I'm so sorry." We rocked back and forth in the swing before he spoke again. His words were slow... thoughtful... hesitant." Many people don't know this, but I had a sister that was older than me."

"Really?" I sniffed and sat up straighter.

"Yeah, five years older than me. She died when I was fourteen."

"Oh."

"We were so close, closer than most. She was the best big sister ever, and she loved being a missionary, she had such a huge heart for the people of Africa."

"How did she," he answered before I could finish.

"She had an undiagnosed heart condition." He began to tear up, and I tried not to concentrate on how amazing his eyes were." It was so unexpected, she seemed fine one day and the next day she just didn't wake up."

"Oh James. I'm so sorry."

"It's okay, I still miss her just as much, it's taken a while to learn how to make it through. Some days are harder than others. The hurt just takes your breath away sometimes, but you make it through, day by day." *Now we're both crying, awesome.*

"I questioned God at first, I didn't know why she had to go so soon. And I still don't know why she died, but I know He had a purpose in it. I still haven't seen it all, but He always has a purpose and one day I'll see it."

"I have to keep reminding myself of that, that he's here and he will heal Carter if it's his will. I just can't imagine life without him."

"I know," he said as he put his arm around me again.

"Thanks for talking, James, it means a lot."

"No problem, I haven't talked to anyone about Lizzie in a while, it was really good for me."

"Lizzie?"

"Well, Elizabeth, but we all called her Lizzie."

"My middle name is Elizabeth."

"Really?"

"Yeah."

I tried to think of something to say but the silence that ensued was comfortable, it seemed to be shared by two of the closest friends. The swing rocked back and forth. Butterflies built in my stomach as I felt his leg against my own.

"Hey, do you know what time it is?" I asked.

"It's after eight!"

"We better go then," I said.

After putting my stuff inside, we headed down the red dusty streets to the orphanage that I had memorized and had grown to love. When we got there, I thought Paige, Dru and Asher were going to lose their minds. There were already several families waiting to be examined and they were having to set everything up by themselves, since the other team had left. Immediately we went into action, filling basins with water and soap, showing each person where to sit as we ran around getting everything ready for the day.

Again, as I knelt down to say hello to the little children who held their mother's hands, they hid their faces behind their mother's skirts. When they were placed in front of me so I could wash their feet, I tickled the bottom of their toes and their faces erupted with laughter. As the smiles grew on their faces and the joy showed through the pain they were experiencing, I thought of Ava. I wanted to be making her smile right about then. About 2:00pm, everything started slowing down and Amber and I went to play with the kids from the orphanage.

Once again my eyes met hers, and her eyes brightened, her lips turning upward into a smile. She immediately ran to me and I scooped her up in my arms. Knowing I couldn't really talk to her, James joined us as we went to play with some other kids.

"How are you?" he asked as we made our way outside to the rest of the children.

"I'm okay. This morning was a good distraction." I looked up at his face and could tell he was genuinely concerned after our heart-to-heart earlier that morning.

"Good," he smiled as two little boys ran up and hugged him around the legs.

Together we played freeze tag for a long time. They had requested to play almost daily after we had taught them how to play a couple weeks ago. Ava played for the first time that day. I could tell, even though she didn't tell me, that something had changed inside of her. I was dying to know her story, know where her parents were, where she lived before she came to the orphanage. I wanted to know all about her. I wanted to know her heart. But she was only two and she couldn't tell me these things; she probably didn't even remember. The rest of the day we all played, laughed, and then played and laughed some more until we had to go back to the guest house.

At the end of the day, laying in my bed reading my Bible, I thought about our trip to the slums, the conversations I'd had with Amber, little Ava, how much I was worried about Carter. Mom had emailed earlier that afternoon saying that while his fever was slowly starting to drop, he was still exhausted and achy. While there was part of me that wanted to be home with him, I was also beginning to see why Carter had fallen in love with this place.

My thoughts were turned to Ava; how much she had come to trust me in the short time that I had known her. The little girl I met the first day was not the little girl I played with today, I was amazed at what a love could do. She had begun to trust me, and each day she opened up a little bit more. She had been a confused, lonely little girl. But now I hoped she could feel a sense of belonging. She didn't have to be lonely anymore because she belonged to a God who loved her.

We set up a clinic the next day. It was full of more families, sweet little girls and boys, and thoughts of Carter. About three o'clock, after I had been bandaging feet all day, we heard the sounds of the blue gates opening and a van driving in.

"Those must be the adoptive families!" Amber said.

"Really?" When the van unloaded, we saw Amber was exactly right, three adoptive families piled out and I saw that some of them had brought some of their own children with them.

"Hey Chrissy, would you like to help us introduce the children to their parents?" Paige asked me.

"I would be honored!" With this, Amber, Paige, one of the nannies, and I headed back to the room where the children were being changed to go meet their parents. One of the families was adopting a two year old little girl, named Aliyah. One was adopting an eighteen month old little girl, named Sonia. And the third was adopting a little boy who was just a little bit over a year named Moses. The nanny handed me the little girl named Sonia and we walked out to introduce the children to their parents. I was reminded of a verse from Psalm, "God sets the lonely in families." All other thoughts were washed away as I began to grasp what was getting ready to happen right before my eyes. In just a few moments these children would know they belonged to a family. They were no longer alone. They now had a mom and dad, sisters and brothers, aunts and uncles, cousins and grandparents. Through these families they would hopefully know the love of God, the same God who had moved mountains to bring them a family.

We walked into a small room filled with nervous faces, awaiting their children. After all of the paperwork and appointments they had done, the moment had finally come. The endless months of waiting were over; they were about to meet their children for the first time. Like most of the rooms in the orphanage it was made of brick, and had a table in the middle onto which all of the families had laid their backpacks. Carrying Sonia in my arms, and seeing her parents with joyous faces, brought tears to my eyes.

The love they already had for this little girl shone in their eyes.

God, you are so evident in this room. What a beautiful miracle this is! Thank you for giving these children families, for adopting them into your family.

I handed her to her father, she looked confused, but her parents were elated. Her mother's eyes were brimming with tears as she watched her husband hold his daughter for the first time. As it had many times already, my heart broke for the children who didn't have families, who weren't going to be loved like little Sonia was. I then thought back to Ava, hopefully she would one day have a family, who would love her with all of their hearts. Her mother's eyes would be full of tears, seeing her for the first time, and her father would hold her with comforting arms. She wouldn't know then that this would be the family to care for her and to love her as long as she lived, but she would someday. She wouldn't know that I had fallen in love with her and would have given anything to make her mine. Even if she never remembered me, even if I couldn't be there forever to love and care for her, I could love on her while I was there, knowing that one day, she would have a family too.

Once they had spent about forty-five minutes with the kids, we had to take the children back to their rooms. The fathers held each of their children in their arms. We led them to their rooms and they placed each of their children back in a bed, where they would sleep

for one of their last nights there. The children once
again had a look of confusion on their faces, wondering
why in the world they had to leave these people.
Sonia's father kissed her on the forehead and walked
out. I watched as their fathers hesitantly left the room.
Aliyah began to throw a fit. A nanny rushed in to
comfort her as I stood with Moses and Sonia. Moses
simply looked around with wide brown eyes, oblivious
to what was happening. I turned to look at Sonia. Her
eyes slowly filled with tears but no sound escaped from
her mouth. I pulled her close as tears blurred my
vision, praying over her.

*Father, help her to know that she belongs, that
these people will be back for her. They are not leaving
her here but are going to love her forever.*

After a full day of washing and bandaging little feet,
I laid in my bed reflecting on my trip thus far. I thought
about how I had changed and how confused I was about
why Carter was so sick. I thought about these children
at the orphanage. They might not have anyone to love
on them when they were sick and had boo-boos. They
had the nannies, who loved them, but they had around
one hundred children to care for daily. One hundred
and fifty children to clothe, feed and care for every
single day. These children came and went; it was not
like the love of a family. While some of these children
would be adopted, some wouldn't. Some people in the
US had the money to adopt, and some didn't. The
heartbreaking reality was most of these children would

194

never be adopted, never have a family, never be loved on by anyone that didn't work at the home. That fact made my heart break, more than it ever had before. I had seen how happy children could be when someone loved them. I had seen how much of a difference it made. I had seen the joy on parent's faces when they were welcoming a much awaited child into their family. What if every child could feel that way? What if every child could be loved by a family? Suddenly the thought hit me, what could I do? What could I do to help every orphaned child feel this way? It was then I realized that what Amber had said was true. Even though Carter was hurt, God was using it for His glory. I had the privilege to come and serve these amazing people. I got to come and pour out my heart in ministering to them, and to think I still had three weeks left; I was in awe of what God was going to do.

Saturday, June 23rd

Today I got to help three children meet their parents for the first time. It was incredible. God is tugging at my heart like never before, He is calling me to do something- I have no idea what. I'm just waiting for Him to guide me. I'm still praying for Carter. Praying God will move in a miraculous way.

Chapter 18

It had been at least a week and a half since I had talked to Hunter. I didn't really want to talk to him after our last conversation and he hadn't tried to contact me either. This resulted in no guilt on my part. Although I hadn't forgotten about him, there were other things occupying my thoughts. I prayed for him and his family often, asking God to show himself to them.

"Mind if I join you?" I asked James that Sunday at church.

"Not at all," he said with a smile, looking at me with his gorgeous blue eyes. I put my Bible and journal down in the chair beside him.

"Hey Chrissy. Can I ask you something?" Ruthie asked me.

"Yes," I said, not knowing what in the world she was going to say.

"Do you have a little sister?" *Why did she want to know?*

But I laughed and responded, "I don't. I have an older brother, and an older sister," thoughts of Carter once again flooded my mind.

I had only gotten a couple updates. From what Mom and Carly had said he was slowly starting to improve.

"Would you like a little sister? I've always thought it would be fun to have a little brother or sister."

She nodded.

I leaned down and whispered in her ear, "But, if you're the baby in the family, you can get away with all kinds of things." We both giggled before the service started. Everyone sang together until the pastor came on stage. Sitting beside James, I noticed something else about him. He could sing, I mean, *really* sing.

Where did that voice come from? I'm pretty sure my insides began to melt a little as I listened to him boldly sing the words of worship and praise.

While the pastor was preaching, my thoughts were everywhere. I was so tired for a number of reasons. It could have been that I was up reading my Bible and praying for answers all night. Or it could have been that I had been in Uganda for almost a month. I was exhausted and just needed a day to relax and maybe catch a nap. All of the sudden my ears perked up, "'Finally, brother, whatever is true, whatever is honorable, whatever is just, whatever is pure, whatever is lovely, whatever is commendable, if there is any excellence if there is anything worthy of praise, think about these things. What you have learned and received and heard and seen in me, practice these things, and the God of peace will be with you. ' Philippians 4:8-9."

It was just as if God had said, "Okay, you're looking for an answer? Here you go. Just honor Me and you will receive peace."

In a room full of people, there was *my* answer, "Whatever is honorable, whatever is pure," and God had chosen to speak to me. The work at the orphanage we were doing at Sole Hope was honorable. My renewed relationship with the Lord was pure. This work I had come to do and grown to love was worthy of praise. My relationship with Hunter wasn't any of these things. I had made a decision to end whatever it was we had left.

That afternoon at about 3:30, I headed up to my room to skype with Hunter, hoping for there to be an email from Mom in my inbox. Not finding an email, I pressed call.

"Hey," he said answering on the third ring.

"Hey, how are you?" I was startled he had answered so quickly. I hadn't expected him to answer at all.

How am I supposed to do this? What in the world am I doing???

"Pretty good. Just starting our day."

"Oh ya'll are in New York, aren't you?" *Great timing Chrissy, really great timing!*

"Yeah. It's great here. Broadway is later today."

198

"Cool. Hey, can we talk?"

"Sure," he looked a little uncomfortable but began to talk, "Hey, I'm sorry I haven't called or Skyped,"

"Listen," I cut him off but had no idea what to say next.

"I'm listening," he laughed.

"I've been doing a lot of thinking, and," I paused again, "I don't think we should keep dating right now."

"What?" He was not happy. At. All.

"I've changed a lot while I've been here."

"Yeah, I've noticed." His remark was full of sarcasm.

"Please, Hunter, let's be honest. This isn't working for either of us. Honestly, I don't think I need to be dating anyone right now." I paused, "My relationship with the Lord has really grown and eventually I need someone beside me who will support that and has the same passion for him. I need to be focusing on Christ and keep my heart pure for the man I'm going to marry one day, the man who will grow alongside of me." *Maybe I shouldn't have said that. Hmm.*

"So, I am assuming that's not me. Right?"

"Um," *What was I supposed to say to that?* "Well, not right now, at least. Not considering where our relationship stood."

"Well, if that's the way you feel, I guess we're finished."

"I'm sorry."

"You know what, I am too. Because I liked the old you a whole lot more before you went on this ridiculous trip anyway." Tears started dripping slowly down my cheeks, *am I really that different?* "Bye." I could hear the loud click of his escape key.

I stared at the black computer screen, watching my mascara run down my face. I realized I wasn't sad our relationship was over, but I was hurt by what he said, "I liked the old you a whole lot more before you went on this ridiculous trip anyway." That hurt. I was pretty sure even I liked myself better now. After a few minutes, having wiped away most of my tears, I walked downstairs to find Amber and Cheryl in the kitchen.

"Hey," Amber said, "Where have you been?"

"Up in my room, skyping Hunter."

"Oh," she said, "Cheryl could we..."

"Of course." Cheryl caught her hint and walked out smiling at me after giving me a quick hug.

"So, have you made a decision?"

I handed her my Bible, opened to Philippians 4, in which verses 8 and 9 were now highlighted in pink.

"Good choice, but a hard one, I know," she said, reading the verses.

"Thanks."

"How did he take it?"

"Well, for starters he told me that he liked me much better before I went on this trip anyway. That pretty much sums up our conversation."

"He didn't take it well?" She said sympathetically.

I sighed, biting into an apple, and sat back down at the table, "Oh, no."

"Well, if it helps I'm sure your whole family is going to love you even more when you get back from this trip, and I am so very proud of you. That was a hard decision. Even if he doesn't like you anymore I think someone else right here in Uganda just might, in fact, I'm pretty positive." She said, and I knew exactly who she was referring to- James Moore. *Blue eyes. Brown hair. Winner smile. Jesus lover.*

"I do not plan on dating anyone presently, thank you."

We both laughed, and walked into the living room together. I had learned that it didn't really matter here if your mascara was smeared on your face- no one would care.

"Hyjack?" James asked us all, walking in with a pack of cards in hand.

He may not care that I have make-up smeared on my face, but I sure do.

I ran up to my room and wiped the make-up off of my face, joining their game five minutes later.

That night after dinner, I went up to my room and emailed Carly.

Carly,
I just want you to know that after some thinking and reading of Philippians 4:8-9, I've broken up with Hunter. Amber and I have been talking and I felt like it

201

was wisest for me to save my heart for the man I will marry someday. Right now I really want to focus on God and my relationship with Him. What do you think? Please send me an update on Carter... haven't heard from Mom in a while.

I pressed send, and opened my journal.

Sunday, July 1st
Philippians 4:8-9, "Finally brother, whatever is true, whatever is honorable, whatever is just, whatever is pure, whatever is lovely, whatever is commendable, if there is any excellence, if there is anything worthy of praise, think about these things. What you have learned and received and heard and seen in me- practice these things, and the God of peace will be with you."

I broke up with Hunter today. Despite knowing I hurt him, I feel a sense of relief knowing I made the right decision. I've only got two more weeks left and while I'm ready to see my family, there's nothing in me that wants to go home. This has been incredible...more than I ever expected.

Two days later, three small children were waiting at the orphanage gates before anyone else, patiently waiting for the doors to open. Like most of the people that came in, their clothes were a bit tattered and they were dirty from the morning breeze kicking up the red dust. Their little feet had no shoes to protect them and we had no way of knowing just how far they had trekked. Paige quickly took them back and sat them down to have their feet worked on. Their feet were some of the worst we had seen yet, with over thirty jiggers on each pair.

"We've got to send somebody home with them so we can instruct their mother on how to care for their feet," Asher said.

"I'll go," I offered, surprising myself.

"You can't go by yourself. Rob will you go with her?" Dru asked.

"Sure," he replied.

Asher explained, in Lugandan, that we would be returning to their house with them to speak with their mother. They nodded. We grabbed a few tubes of antibiotic cream, some gauze rolls and the children started showing us the way to their house. They looked to be about 3, 5, and 8 years old. We walked down the main road for quite some time and then turned down a bunch of back streets that we hoped would take us to where we needed to be. I didn't know how we were going to manage to find our way back. After a solid forty-five minute journey in the blazing heat, we arrived at their home, greeted by their mother who had been eagerly awaiting their arrival.

"Asante sana," their mother said with grateful eyes after we did our best to tell her how to care for her children's feet. I had figured out by this point that she had just told us "Thank you very much." For the first time since stepping into their home, I allowed my eyes to scan the small hut. A large pot and a single pan near the fire: Two wooden spoons, a small collection of food and two cushions stacked up against the far wall. The children immediately ran back out of the house to go back to work. Their mother gathered half of the scarce food supply and began to prepare a meal, all while having a baby tied to her back. *This is how they live. Cook, work, eat, work, sleep, and do it all over again*, I thought to myself.

I had seen the slums and while their conditions were far worse, the lifestyle was similar. I had expected, hoped, that the way they lived was only the case inside the slums. But I was wrong. That way of living was everywhere, it was common. If I had been born in here, this would have been my life as well.

There these children were, heading to the dump, looking for small bits of scrap metal to sell for a few shillings. Children are supposed to play, and make messes with toys, not work all day in the hot sun like these children were. While making the long walk back to the orphanage I saw many more children just like the ones we walked home. When we got back to the orphanage it was about time to go play with the kids. Dozens of families had come in, Paige told us they had worked on at least fifty people that morning.

It didn't occur to me until I was playing with Ava that afternoon that I had changed even more than her

204

since I had arrived. The Lord had shaped my heart and turned me into a completely different person than I had been just three weeks ago. I knew when I got back home all my friends would be talking about the Broadway shows and the shopping they did. All I would have to do was look back and hope I made a lasting impression for others and for God's kingdom. He had chosen to use me, a seventeen year old girl, to do his work and bring glory to his name.

The words Carter had said to me right before I left played over and over again in my head, "This will be so much better than some trip to New York." Because when I got home, I would know I loved children who needed to be loved. I had changed a life; made an impact on at least one person. That was what made me realize that this trip was much, much more important than seeing Broadway shows in New York. Hunter was right. I had changed, but it was definitely for the better.

Tuesday, July 3rd

Today, three little kids came to the orphanage to get their feet worked on. Rob and I walked them home. They lived in a tiny hut, barely big enough for someone to walk around in. Their mother thanked us, and we left to come back. I realized today how different I really am. Hunter was right, I've changed, but I know that the way I have changed will make an impact on things that are everlasting.

The next morning I opened my computer expectantly, hoping to find an email from my mom in my inbox. I was not disappointed, but my heart began to beat faster as I clicked on the email.

Chrissy,
We are in the middle of running more blood tests to see if the infection is going down. His fever is dropping. And he says that the pain is decreasing along with the aching in his body. So we're making progress- slowly. Carly told us about you and Hunter. We know that was hard, but we are so proud that you followed what God was calling you to do. We can't wait to see you. I'll try and skype you tomorrow, honey. I love you and miss you. Can't wait to hear your stories. Keep praying sweetheart.
    Love you,
    Mom

I was so relieved just to have him a little bit better... better than before.

"James?" I yelled running through the house after I had showered, "James?" I found him on the back porch reading his bible.

"Need something?" He asked with a smile on his face as I peeked my head out the back door and went and sat down beside him on the swing.

"Not really, just wanted to tell you that I got an email from my mom."

206

"And?"

"His fever is going down, and the pain is decreasing."

"That's awesome. I've been praying."

"But they are running more tests to see if the infection has gone down, so we'll see how much better he actually is when the results come back."

"Then we will keep praying. Chrissy, I'm just glad he's getting better."

"Me too, lifts such a burden off of my shoulders."

"I can imagine, you haven't been yourself the past few days. I've been worried about you." He placed his hand on top of mine for just a moment.

His words played over in my head. *I've been worried about you.* Had he been thinking about me as much as I had been thinking about him?

"Thanks, James. It will be a lot different from now on."

"We better get going," he said with a smile, and with that we went inside to eat breakfast before starting another long day.

Chapter 19

"Hey Chrissy!" Paige came up to me a few days later while I was playing with Ava after lunch.

"Hey!"

"I have a project for you," she announced.

"Okay," I stood up and put Ava on my hip.

"When the last mission group was here their main purpose was updating the orphanage, but there was one room they ran out of time to paint after they sanded it."

"So," I added as she paused.

"So I was wondering if you, James and Amber could paint it. I would do it but we're heading out soon to take the current Sole Hope team to the market."

"Sure. Where's the paint?"

"There's a couple of cans in the storage room. You may have to dig around a bit to find it."

"All right, thanks. Oh, what room do you want us to paint?"

"I'll show you."

Before walking off she turned to Asher who was inspecting the foot of a young mother, "I'll be right back."

She led me to one of the two dining rooms for the children. I could tell why she needed us to paint it. The walls were bare since they had already sanded. After she showed me I went and found James, he was still washing a child's foot.

"Hey," I said, sitting on the stool beside him.

"Hey, how are you?" James asked.

"Good. You wanna help me with something?"

"Of course," he smiled at me, wiping his hands on his worn khaki shorts.

"Paige needs us to paint one of the rooms; the room the older kids eat in."

"All right," He picked up the little boy who had been placed in front of him and sat him down in front of Dru so he could remove the jiggers in his feet.

"We'll be back in a little bit," he told Dru and then turned to me, "Where's the paint?

"In here," I motioned to the storage room where boxes of supplies were piled high to the ceiling. On one side of the room the orphanage had stored donations like sheets, blankets and clothes for the children. The opposite wall was lined with boxes from Sole Hope filled with gauze and soap for the clinics. In the back was a collection of miscellaneous items where I assumed the paint was. It smelled of the same medicated soap we used each day for foot washing.

But of course, like every room in the orphanage, it was sticky and hot due to the lack of air conditioning.

"Ought to be fun to find." His eyes went wide.

"Yeah."

"Well, let's get started." We started moving the bulky boxes aside so we could get to the back of the small room. After twenty minutes of hunting we finally found two cans of light blue paint and some worn brushes.

"Let's get to work," he said as we headed to the dining room to start painting. As we painted, I heard James start humming a song I knew quite well. But it was different than usual. In the orphanage all of the nannies taught the children "Jesus Loves Me" in their language. You could hear it ringing through the halls every day. It was beautiful to hear these children singing about how God loved them, because he was the only father some of them would ever know.

As James was humming, and we were both painting, I found myself joining him. A few seconds later several of the older children walked in for dinner, they heard me singing and joined in.

We sang the words over and over and over again. Suddenly more and more children filled the room and it was like a choir. Because they had nowhere else to eat, the kids gathered inside and we just kept on singing. Tears started filling my eyes; it was the most beautiful sound I had ever heard. A single tear fell down my cheek, but I rushed to wipe it away before James noticed. It didn't work.

"You okay?" he asked, his lips turning up into a smile.

I nodded as another tear dripped down my cheek. I picked my paintbrush back up and started to paint again, trying to keep my eyes from getting too puffy.

James and I looked at each other and smiled at Amber as she walked in.

"What's going on in here?" She said quietly, "Did you start this?"

"Well," I said, wiping away the last of my tears.

"Not purposefully," he finished for me.

"It's beautiful. They could go on tour," she replied, shocked.

James looked over at me, then the children and smiled. There was something so different about him.

After we got back from the orphanage that day, I couldn't take my mind off of James. I had dreamed my whole life of finding a guy like him but now I was conflicted with all kinds of new emotions. What was I supposed to do? I had already told myself now wasn't the time to date. God had changed my heart and I thought I had everything figured out. But I was so wrong, everything was all mixed up again.

Carly-

He's so very different. The way he cares about people, the way he respects me, the way he plays with

211

kids, the way he loves Jesus. But I don't feel like I should be dating anyone right now. He doesn't seem like he wants to date... and hasn't brought it up. But I feel like he will at some point. I'm leaving in two short weeks and I need advice on what to do.

"Hey Amber," I said walking into the kitchen where she was cooking dinner.

"Hey," she said, looking up at me from her recipe book, "You need to talk?"

"Um," I was trying to figure out how to phrase this, "So, I broke up with Hunter for two reasons. First, he wasn't helping me grow spiritually. If anything, he was hindering me. The other reason was that I agreed with what you said, that I just simply didn't need to be dating right now."

"Those are both great reasons, but you seem to have a little extra sparkle in your eye ever since..."

I interrupted with, "Since James came, I know." I couldn't help but smile, "That's my problem. I still feel committed to not date, but I just don't know what to do, or how to handle it," I folded my head on my crossed arms already resting the table and sighed.

"Just because someone loves the Lord and your circumstances have changed doesn't mean that what God told you before is not still true for you now."

I propped my head on my hands, listening to what she had to say.

"It's not that James isn't wonderful in many ways,"

I smiled. *So many ways.*

"But God told you before that this is not the season in your life to be dating. In fact you said yourself, you didn't think that had changed. I have no doubt that you'll know that the person and the time are right when God brings a godly man into your life. I wasted a lot of time dating in high school and college trying to force a relationship to work, but when the time was right God literally placed Rob right in front of me. There was no forcing or questioning. I just knew in my heart that it was the right time."

"But I've never met anyone like him. He just seems so perfect."

"It's perfectly okay to spend time with him and enjoy his company, there's nothing wrong with that. You'll just have to decide for yourself what type of relationship will be the most honoring to God for the two of you right now."

I laughed, "I'm certainly getting ahead of myself."

"Why is that?"

"He's never told me how he feels about me."

"I'm pretty sure we all can tell," Amber said as she turned back to preparing supper, "And you never know, maybe he'll come back into the picture one day. You never know what God has planned."

Her words repeated in my head as I walked upstairs to shower before dinner, "*You never know what God has planned.*" Oh, how true that had become, and how exciting it would be for my future.

"Hey everybody! How are you?" My parents skyped me that Sunday. It was after church my time but they had just started their day. I could see they were at the hospital.

"We're fine, how are you sweetie?" my mom asked.

"I'm great. How's Carter?"

"Sleeping a lot," Mom responded.

"He's getting really tired of sitting all day," Carly said, like she was the one going through all of this.

"I bet he's going stir crazy," I said.

"Oh, trust me. You have no idea," they responded.

"What does he do all day?"

"Mostly watch TV and sleep, the results came back."

"And?"

"The infection is slowly going down."

"Good. We're all praying here."

Carly turned to Mom, Dad and Carter, and whispered something and then turned back to me, "Sorry I didn't respond to your email."

"It's okay, I took care of it," I could see she was taking the laptop somewhere, "Where are you going?"

"Out in the hallway."

"Why?"

"So we can talk. I pretty sure you don't want to talk about boys with Mom, Dad and Carter, right?"

"Right." I didn't know where she was going with this.

"So how did you take care of it?" She asked, making quotation marks with her fingers around the words, *take care of it.*

"I talked to Amber, we've had a lot of good conversations."

"About?"

"Life, boys...God."

"What did she say about it?"

"That I needed to trust my instinct from the beginning and just not date right now, and if that's what I felt like God was calling me to do two weeks ago, then I needed to stick with that. She said it's okay to enjoy his company and be friends but just to make the wisest decisions concerning our relationship."

"Good, I didn't really have anything really smart or grown up sounding to tell you, so I'm glad you talked to her."

"Me too, sorry I went so long without skyping, we've just been really busy."

"I understand, and I'll tell Mom and Dad."

"Is Carter really doing okay?"

"He's okay, I guess. Still in a lot of pain. The infection is going down, but it's just hard to see him like this."

"I know...I wish I could be there with you all."

"No you don't. You love it there! I can see it in your face." I smiled at that. It was true.

"You're right. I do. It's been more than amazing."

"He talks about you every day, and asks how you are doing. He checks his email like every hour to see if you've emailed. He really misses you."

"We have the best big brother ever."

"So true."

"I need to go help Amber with dinner. I'll skype again soon, I promise."

"Okay, love you, miss you!" She said as we both logged off.

Sunday, July 8th

Today we went to church, and I skyped with the family this afternoon. It was so good to talk to them. I'm really missing them – but not ready to go home quite yet – and don't think I'll ever be ready to leave. Amber and I had a really good conversation about James and that whole situation. We both agreed that I said before I didn't think it was the right time for me to be dating and that it still applies now. Ava is doing well, cute as ever, I'm praying so hard that she will get a wonderful family one day very soon. Still praying for God to heal Carter completely so he can come back. I can't wait to see what God is going to do in my life – much less hers, but I'm getting impatient already!

The next day I woke up bright and early, ready to face the day, whatever it may bring.

"Good morning, Chrissy, you seem to be in a good mood this morning," Cheryl said as I came into the kitchen that Monday morning, while she was fixing Ruthie a bowl of cereal.

"Good morning, and thanks," I said sticking my head in the fridge.

"How did you sleep last night?"

It was so cool how we were all like one big family.

"Great, how about you?"

"Pretty good, Stephen's snoring kept me up, but I'm used to it."

I laughed and then sat down at the table to eat my breakfast before walking over to the orphanage.

Once I was finished, we all walked over together and I snuck back into Ava's room before the morning crowd got there.

"Hey there, cutie," I said finding her crib, and lifting her up into my arms, hugging a few of the other kids. She held tight to me as I took her into the breakfast room where all of the other kids were gathered to eat.

"I'll be back," I whispered in her ear as I sat her down to eat and I walked back out to help with whatever needed to be done for the clinic. When I got to the storage room, no one was in there. I checked the room where the clinics were held, still, I found no one. I heard engines from outside though. So I walked out to where the noises were and found all of the adoptive families gathered together taking pictures of several trucks in the main yard. They were piled high with sack cloths and barrels.

"What's going on?" I walked over to talk to Amber, who was also taking pictures.

"All of the adoptive families have paid for the orphanage to have extra fruit, rice, flour, beans, and sugar. When the adoptive families come, they always buy supplies for the orphanage, but the fruit is more of a treat since they don't get it very often."

"Wow, how amazing." I could see James was walking over towards me, and my heart beat faster the closer he got.

"That's awesome," he said gazing over towards the supplies.

"Yeah," I said and then let out a short sigh. *And again, why wasn't I going to date him?*

"These kids at the orphanage will be so blessed with what they have been able to do."

"Not only that, but the kids they are adopting, too."

"I can't imagine. Their lives will be changed forever."

"They were probably so confused at the beginning."

"Oh yeah," his blue eyes looked heavy, "But they will be loved forever, how amazing that God can turn one desire of a husband and wife into a child being loved forever."

"And then it's like a domino effect. One child is adopted and as they grow they have a heart for orphans. It just keeps going and going." I looked up at him. His blue eyes locked on mine and it seemed as if time stood still.

I forced myself to look back at the trucks, look at the orphanage children, focus on something besides this boy with the blue eyes.

"Incredible what he can do," James concluded.

I glanced over to see the families with their new children. The mothers held their children in their arms, smiles on their faces. They were smiles of trust, smiles of laughter, smiles of children who had families. They were now children who would have a mother to hold them when they cried, fathers to pick them up and dust them off when they were hurt. These were children who were going to be taught about a God who is merciful and forgiving, and who can turn your life around in seconds. And oh, how I wished Ava was one of these children.

Chapter 20

I was sitting on the back step of the orphanage after a game of soccer with some of the older kids, taking a break before our next game. My hair was in a sloppy pony tail that I had thrown up mid game, and I wiped the sweat off my forehead when James called out my name. My heart fluttered. He came and sat down beside me and after asking me how my day had been, began to say, "I always knew I would end up on the mission field, and from the beginning I knew that would narrow down the selection of girls who would be interested in living that kind of life, because it's not always easy."

And here comes the conversation I had been waiting for. My heart began to race. *How does his hair still look so good? And wow, his eyes are especially blue today.*

"But when I met you, I could tell, even from our first conversation at the supper table, that you were interested in missions and that your heart was so completely focused on Jesus."

I just decided I wouldn't get into a relationship. This definitely sounds like it's going in that direction.

"I need to be honest, I wasn't like that until this trip. My heart began to change just a few short days before you arrived. I was really consumed with all of the things that come along with high school. Boyfriend, shopping, parties, nothing to really do with God. He was kind of in the back of my mind. Until now. He's broken my heart and put it back together like I never could have imagined. I now have a heart for so many things I didn't before. He's changed me to the point that I don't even think," I paused doubting what I was about to say, "dating is something I need to be doing right now. I'm not saying it's never going to happen. But a close friend who loves the Lord is something I desperately need right now."

"Oh," was all that he said. Moments later he broke the silence, "I can handle waiting."

I looked down at the floor, not believing what I had just said, the nervous feeling stopped, but the fluttering didn't. *Did I just turn away the guy who seemed to be so perfect? What if he finds someone else before I'm ready to move past "friend zone?"*

"I really respect and admire you for being so truthful and up front with me, but it doesn't change at all how I feel about you," he said.

221

He's so wonderful. His heart is just amazing, and look at those eyes! It would be so much easier just to kiss him right now. Chrissy stop.

Lord, I need a sign that I'm making the right decision.

"And just because it's not the right timing, doesn't mean I don't feel the same way." *Should I tell him?* "Because I do," I confessed.

There's that grin! And how he looks at me with those eyes! I paused and then continued.

"I just feel like there is something else God has in store for both of us right now." I paused, yet again, "But what do we do with how we feel?"

"We just keep our eyes focused on Christ."

Focused on Christ. Thank you, Lord.

"Until it's the right time for both of us, for now we can be just friends," I said continuing his thought.

"Agreed. Not that you were wondering, but I think you are beautiful, *inside* and out."

"Even with a sweaty, sloppy pony tail?"

"Especially with a sweaty, sloppy pony tail."

"And I'm amazed at your heart for Christ daily, oh, and your eyes?" I paused, "They're perfect," I giggled and my cheeks turned as pink as my t-shirt.

"Friends?" James said flashing his smile, locking his eyes on mine and holding out his hand for me to take.

"Friends," I said, placing my hand in his. A sense of peace filled my heart. A peace that I knew was supposed to be there. A peace I had been looking for since I hit the red dirt of Uganda in that airplane.

Tuesday, July 10th

James and I talked earlier today. We both made the decision that this isn't the time for us to date. It was so hard for both of us to make that decision, but we know God has something else in store for both of us right now. He's such the perfect guy with such a wonderful heart and I hope that one day...just one day when God's timing is right, we will be together.

I was trying not to count the days down to when I had to leave- but it was six. Six days until I had to leave this country I had grown to love so much. Six days until I had to leave Ava. Six days until I had to leave Amber, Rob, and James. Six days until I had to go back to normal life in America. Six days for God to heal Carter before I came home, because I knew He would, but for some reason, I was still worried. I was dreading that day when I would have to walk onto the plane and fly home.

"Good morning," I said walking down in the kitchen the next morning.

"Morning," Amber said in return, turning on the water in the sink to wash some dishes.

"James and I talked yesterday."

"Really?"

"Yep."

"And, how did it go?" She asked eagerly, turning towards me.

"Well, he totally professed his love for me, or something like that," I blushed.

"Oh my."

"Yeah, I simply told him that I didn't feel like it was the right time for us to be dating and he agreed after I gave my reasons."

"Good," Amber said, turning around with dishes in hand and a bubbles covering her fingers.

"The hardest thing is that we both feel the same way about each other."

"What are you going to do?" She had completely stopped all dishwashing and was entirely tuned into our conversation.

"We are going to keep our eyes focused on Christ and wait for God's timing and see what He has in store."

"You both made the best decision and I'm very proud of you."

"Thanks. It means a lot."

"Oh, we better go. Grab something quick for breakfast and we'll head out," she said looking at the clock, seeing it was after eight thirty, almost nine. We started walking to the orphanage, talking the whole way there. But all I could think about was the fact that I only had six days left.

When we got back that afternoon, there was an email in my inbox. The nerves piled up in the pit of my stomach as I clicked open the email.

Chrissy-

OUR LORD IS AMAZING! We did more blood tests yesterday the infection is GONE! They are sending us home in two days with medicine to continue to treat him!!! We will be home in time for you to get back! Praise God from whom all blessings flow!

Once again my eyes filled with tears as I sat at my desk. *God, thank you. Thank you. Thank you. Thank you. You are incredible. And I love you. I love you more than a boy, more than this life, more than anything. Thank you for bringing this family back to life. Thank you for moving this summer in ways we would have never imagined. In ways I never even asked for!*

"James! James!" I shouted running through the house and down the stairs, even though it was after nine.

"What?" He said coming out of his room with basketball shorts and a t-shirt on.

"The infection," I was out of breath. I grabbed his arms, "is gone! He's going home in two days!"

He wrapped me in his arms and we stood in the hall together until Amber came down, "What was all that about?" She asked laughing.

I pulled out of our hug and said, "The infection is gone!"

"Are you serious?"

"Of course I am! My mom emailed me today."

"Oh, Chrissy." She embraced me in a hug.

"I knew He would heal him," I said.

"We all did," James replied, smiling at me.

Chapter 21

It went by in a flash. Suddenly my trip was coming quickly to a close.

We went one last time to the slums to do a clinic, we were able to work on at least four dozen feet that day. We had started off with hundreds of children to work with, and we never thought we would be able to work on all of their feet, but we had done it! When we pulled in, the children were so happy to see our car packed full with supplies to do a clinic. Their faces lit up with smiles as we unloaded and began the last clinic. The end of that day was bittersweet for all of us. Our work there, for now, was over. We had come to know and love so many of these people and I would miss days spent with all of these children.

My flight didn't leave until seven at night, so I spent all day at the orphanage, loving on the kids I had grown so close to, especially Ava. I was going to miss her so very much. We played one last game of soccer with the boys and James. Embracing Ava snugly in my arms, I made her a promise. I would be back to see her. I kissed her forehead and sat her down to eat dinner.

"Bye," I walked over and hugged Paige.

"Bye," she replied, "Thank you so much."

"I loved every minute of it," I responded, starting to tear up.

"We would love to have you back."

"Don't worry, I'll be back," I said confidently.

"Good," we hugged once again and I waved goodbye to everyone at the orphanage as James, Amber, Rob and I got in the car and pulled out. As we drove down the road, I saw the mud huts and mothers with babies on their backs for the last time. My thoughts drifted back to my very first car ride in Uganda. Oh how different my thoughts had been then. I had only seen the dirt and the old clothes on people's backs. Now my perspective had drastically changed; while I still saw the tattered clothing on their backs, it was out of compassion and not in judgment. I knew there wasn't much they could do about their current situations. But that didn't mean I couldn't strive to make a difference.

When we arrived at the airport three hours later, I slung my backpack on my shoulder, and James rolled my suitcase into the airport. After finding the check in area, it was time to say my final goodbyes. I hugged Amber, and fought back the tears knowing I wouldn't be able to keep them back for long.

"Bye, friend," I said.

"We're gonna miss you," she said sadly.

"I'm gonna miss you too." *And there they come.*

"Don't forget to come back and see us," she said as I gave Rob a hug.

"Don't worry, I won't." With this, James embraced me. I breathed in deeply so I could carry his scent with me on the flight home. I leaned my head back and memorized the exact blue of his eyes. He kissed me on the forehead, and I couldn't find any words as his tears fell into my hair.

"Bye," was all he said and he wiped the tears off of my cheeks.

"I'll miss you."

"I'll miss you, too, be safe."

"I will," I said with a smile." Well, I better go," I added as I grabbed my suitcase. With one more hug from James and Amber I walked off waving goodbye; wiping my face on my shirt sleeve. I was devastated to leave my now beloved country.

Once I was on the plane, I tried to read a book I had brought with me, but it was no use. All I could think about was Ava, James, of course, Uganda and everything else it held dear to me, everything I had learned there. I worried that Ava would think I forgot all about her, that I didn't care about her. I wished that there was some way I could have shown her how much I loved her. I hoped that she would grow up knowing the love of God. Even if she never knew the love of a family, she could know the love of God and that would be enough. With that thought in mind, as I looked out the window at the red dirt of the country I now loved so deeply, tears ran down my cheek, but soon I found myself falling into a deep, comforting sleep.

A couple of ridiculously long flights, several movies and three airplane meals later, I awoke to the sound of the pilot on the intercom and was relieved to be landing soon. I couldn't wait to see my family but I wished I was back in Uganda spending the day at the orphanage with Ava and James. A day washing feet and playing with children sounded ten times better than a day at the mall.

"Ladies and gentlemen, we are nearing Raleigh, North Carolina. Please fasten your seat belts and stay seated until the seatbelt sign has been turned off."

Forty minutes later we were on the ground in Raleigh. I walked off of the plane and down the hall, well, more like ran, and then I could see them waiting with a sign that said, "Welcome home Chrissy! We missed you!" Even Nathan, Carly's boyfriend had come.

I bolted the rest of the way, and ran directly into my mom's wide open arms.

"Chrissy," Carter said, sitting on a bench close by. I walked over to him, he pulled me close and we sat speechless for a few minutes. He was a miracle, and I was so happy that I was sitting with him. I was reminded why I had gone to Uganda in the first place, and how I had come back so changed. After my little love fest with the rest of the family we got my luggage, and headed back home.

"How was your trip?" Carter asked.

"Incredible. I saw and learned so much. Amber and Rob were great, made me feel at home the whole time. There was this little girl named Ava..." I went on and on until we pulled into the driveway of our home, 476 Collie Circle in my sweet town of Holly Springs, NC.

When we walked in I found another "Welcome Home" poster in my room, my room that was twice the size of a home in Uganda. Mom had fixed my favorite meal for dinner: chicken casserole with baked potatoes. I was unpacking some of my stuff after I had taken a shower and decided to go talk to Carter for a few minutes downstairs in the living room.

"I just wanted to say thanks." I sat down beside him on the couch.

"For what?" He asked, puzzled.

"Making me go. It was truly incredible."

"I knew it would be a great experience for you."

"It really opened up my eyes to understand the basic needs and struggles that so many people go through every single day."

"That happened with me too when I went during Christmas break of my sophomore year in college, how did everything with Sole Hope go?"

"Really well, there were dozens of families and children that came every day. We went to the slums three days to do clinics and pass out dresses. Rob and I actually walked three kids back to their home after they came to the clinic."

"That's really cool, where did they live?"

"In the middle of nowhere. Their house was so small, especially for all of those people that lived there. What shocked me was that almost all of those people lived like that."

"In almost all of Uganda people who don't live in the city live in situations like that, I'm sure you saw that."

"I loved Amber, we had some really good conversations."

"Oh yeah, about what?"

"Just life. How are Carly and Nathan?"

"Really good actually, getting serious."

"Really? I didn't expect that coming."

"None of us did, they've only been dating a few months."

"Well, that means I must check this all out with Carly," I said walking out of the living room, and heading back upstairs to get the low down from my sister.

"Carly, can I come in?" I asked, knocking on her door.

"Of course." I walked in and plopped down on her bed beside her.

"James and I talked."

"Really?" She scooted closer to me on the bed.

"Yeah."

"Do you have a boyfriend?"

"Nope."

"Oh."

"Yeah, and what makes it worse is that he totally laid his heart out for the taking, and then I told him I felt the exact same way, but said I didn't feel like now was the time for us to be dating."

"What did he say?"

"After I gave my reasoning, he agreed and we are both going to focus on Christ until we feel like it is God's timing for us to be together."

"Ya'll are smart."

"Thanks," I said smiling, "How are you and Nathan?"

"Really good, he's different than any other guys I've dated. I can tell he really does love me, but more than that he keeps his relationship with God first." She paused." I'm sorry I haven't confided more in you about this but it seems crazy to me sometimes, how serious it's getting so quickly."

"I just want to be there for you like you've always been there for me." I yawned." But right now I've got to go to bed. I can't keep my eyes open."

Her eyes met mine as I stood to walk to my room, "Thank you, Chrissy. You better keep your eyes open for a few more steps so you don't run into something. Goodnight, I'm so glad you are home."

"Love you," I shouted walking into my room, crawling into my bed without even changing out of my clothes.

Chapter 22

I had been home for three days. It was Sunday, and I was actually excited that we were going to church as a family. I got up around seven that morning and enjoyed a long, hot shower. I was still amazed every time I turned the faucet on and hot water came out on demand. I then took the time to fix my hair, something I hadn't really done in six weeks.

After the service was over, I headed to Sunday School, and was immediately greeted by Natalie, just like always.

"Hey girl! Where have you been? We missed you," She asked me.

"No one told you?"

"Told me what?"

"I went to Uganda to serve for six weeks, since Carter couldn't go."

"Are you serious?" Her eyes went wide. The shock in her voice was understandable." That's amazing Chrissy. How was it?"

"Fantastic. I had such an amazing time and learned so much."

"We should have breakfast together soon so you can tell me about it."

"We should! I'll text you this week and we can work something out. Would you mind sharing a little something this morning?"

"I'd love to." With this we walked into our classroom. I took a spot beside a girl named Megan, her blonde hair was curly today and fell just below her shoulders. I had talked with her only a few times before, but she really seemed glad I was there.

"Hey, Chrissy, how are you?" she turned to me and asked.

"I'm great, and you?"

"Pretty good. We've missed having you these last couple of weeks," she said pulling her pocket sized Bible from her purse.

"I've missed being here. I was actually in Uganda for six weeks."

"Really?" I could tell she, too, was shocked.

"Yeah. My brother Carter and I got in a car wreck,"

"I heard about that. We've been praying for him."

"Thank you. But yeah, I went in his place. It ended up being absolutely amazing."

"How cool," she said." I'm hoping to go somewhere next summer. Not really sure where yet though."

Natalie interrupted our conversation.

236

"Good morning guys. Chrissy just got back from Uganda and she's going to share a little bit about her trip with us before we get going." Natalie smiled and motioned to me.

"So, first of all, I'd like to thank you all for praying for my brother, Carter. He is doing so much better since the car wreck and it's been such an answer to prayers. He was supposed to go back to Uganda six weeks ago but he couldn't because of the wreck. I went for him for six weeks. I was absolutely dreading it beforehand.

"But over the last six weeks God did some pretty incredible things in my heart. I was moved to such great compassion towards the people and children of Uganda. There was one little girl in particular, Ava, who I got really close to. She was brought into the orphanage while I was there. I think I might have a picture," I took my phone from the side of my purse and brought up a picture of Ava and me outside one day. I handed it to Megan and she passed it around the room.

"Anyway, while we were there we worked with Sole Hope removing jiggers and doing clinics within the orphanage and in the slums. Their conditions are heartbreaking and I honestly can't imagine living like that. It was a hard six weeks but one that I wouldn't have missed it for the world. God moved so mightily in my life and He's become more important to me than ever." I paused and looked around the room. Natalie's eyes were glossed over with tears threatening and Megan was smiling at me.

"Wow. Thank you," Natalie began, "Today we're going to be in Romans 12, more specifically verse 12." I turned to the passage and listened to the sound of pages turning.

"Megan, would you read it please?" Natalie asked.

"Sure," Megan cleared her throat and began, "Rejoice in hope, be patient in tribulation, be constant in prayer."

Natalie let the importance of this verse hang in the air for a moment before speaking.

"I've often turned to this verse when I need a reminder of what I need to be doing as a follower of Christ. Though it's three simple phrases, they are three very important phrases. Rejoice in hope. Be patient in tribulation. Be constant in prayer.

"First, I'd like us to look at another verse about hope in Hebrews six. Chrissy, would you mind reading verses eighteen and nineteen?"

I nodded and turned to the passage, "So that by two unchangeable things, in which it is impossible for God to lie, we who have fled for refuge might have strong encouragement to hold fast to the hope set before us. We have this as a sure and steadfast anchor of the soul, a hope that enters into the inner place behind the curtain."

"This hope we have in Christ is greater than anything we will ever face. You guys are going into your Senior year. This is a big year in which you will be faced with a lot of decisions to make. You'll have days you will have to be purposeful in being patient in tribulation and you will have to hold tight to this hope in Christ.

"And in those moments, being constant in prayer is key."

How did I sit here for all of these years and not pay attention to these conversations? They are life-changing.

I stayed after Sunday School and talked to Megan and Natalie. We planned to meet to have coffee for breakfast on Tuesday morning. Together we walked upstairs and went our separate ways. I met everyone else at the car and we drove home for lunch.

"How was Sunday School, Chrissy?" Mom asked during lunch.

"Really good, actually," I replied, "Megan and Natalie are meeting me for breakfast on Tuesday."

That night Carter, Carly and I played "Disney Sing It: Family Hits" edition for a while, which was extremely entertaining and got my mind off of missing Uganda. I headed up to my room at about 10:00, and my phone was playing music announcing a call.

"Hello," I said, picking it up.

"Hey Chrissy, its Audrey!"

"Hey girl. How are you?"

"Really good, how was Uganda, totally terrible, right?" she scoffed, but it made my stomach churn. *Was I really* that *shallow before Uganda?*

"Actually it was amazing and such an awesome experience. You should come with me next time I go."

"Wow, next time? I wasn't expecting that. I thought you were totally dreading it. What happened?" She seemed bewildered.

"I was dreading it, but when I got there God really opened my eyes about how shallow I was living my life. You wouldn't believe the conditions these people live in. It's insane. Through a bunch of experiences there my entire relationship with the Lord was completely renewed. He actually led me to make some pretty drastic changes."

"Changes? What kind of changes?"

"Well for starters I broke up with Hunter a couple of weeks ago."

"What?" She said surprised, I could picture her in my mind, her eyes wide with shock, but reapplying mascara and lip-gloss at the same time.

"I broke up with Hunter."

"Why?"

"First, he wasn't going to church ever, and his relationship with God obviously wasn't the most important thing in his life," I tried to explain.

"Oh. I guess I see where you are coming from, how did you do it?"

"Really Audrey?"

"What?"

"Over skype, how else would I do it from Uganda?"

"How did he take it?"

"Not too well. He said he liked me more before I went on the trip anyway."

"Snap. I guess he didn't take it as well as you had hoped."

"Nope. I mean I didn't think he would be all rainbows and butterflies about it. How was New York?"

"Oh my gosh! It was absolutely incredible. We had such a great time. Wait, when did you break up with Hunter?"

"Um, I don't know. Right when ya'll had gotten to New York, why?"

"He was in a horrible mood the whole time. That would explain it."

"Yeah." I couldn't help but feel a bit guilty for ruining his trip.

"Well, just thought I would check in on you. We need to hang out soon, okay?"

"Okay, love you girl. Bye."

"Right back atcha'." With this she hung up and I opened my lap top so I could email Amber.

Amber,

Missing you my friend! Everyone is doing well, but I'm not quite over the jet lag just yet. Carter is feeling so much better. He doesn't look completely broken

241

anymore. Have you been able to see Ava? How are Dru and Asher? And everything with Sole Hope? Thank you so much for everything, I've been keeping you all in my prayers.

With much love,
Chrissy

After sending it, I closed my laptop, changed into my pajamas and crawled into bed, hoping to wake up refreshed from the lingering jet-lag.

The words my youth minister spoke that Wednesday night were so perfect, "I've said this before, and you're probably tired of hearing it, but God has given you all of the tools to do miraculous things. All you have to do is have faith that He will do it. But in order for these things to happen, some changes may be necessary. You may have to drop some activities, maybe change some ways you do certain things in your life. Now I've been a youth minister for almost eight years and I have learned to see it. I can see it in your eyes, when you are struggling, when God is tugging on your heart. When you are being convicted to do something so strongly that the feeling just won't go away, sometimes God wants things to happen that require changes, that require faith, but you have to trust Him. Through the power of the Holy Spirit He's given you all of the tools to do extraordinary things." I soaked in the words, it was like God was affirming everything I had felt in Uganda. Throughout my whole trip, I knew

God was calling me to do something more. To be more than I was before. I now, for the first time, wanted to be who God wanted me to be. This trip had become so much more than filling in Carter's spot for a month. Just like Amber said, God had planned it, He had ordained it from the beginning.

After we had gotten home from church, I was listening to music on my laptop in my room while I spent some time in the Bible.

My computer beeped from across the room.

Who wants to Skype?

My heart beat faster, hoping it was James. It was.

"Hey!" I said grinning.

"I've missed you," his blue eyes brightened.

He's missed me!

"I've missed you, too."

"How are you?" He propped his head up on his elbow.

"I'm great. Definitely missing Uganda."

"How's Carter?" I could see that he was sitting in the living room with the lights on. It was pitch-black outside.

"He's doing really well. He's hoping to come back within the next two months."

"I can't wait to meet him."

"I've told him a lot about you."

"Oh no," he laughed.

"All good things. No need to worry," I smiled back at him." How are you?"

"Well, the house is a little boring without you."

I blushed.

"I went to see Ava yesterday, actually. Here, I'll send you a picture." I waited as he sent a picture over from his phone to the computer." It should be there any second."

I saw the email icon flash seconds later. The picture showed him pushing Ava on the swings at the orphanage. He was wearing a navy blue t-shirt with khaki shorts and his classic, charming grin, the one I adored. Ava's face was filled with a smile as she swung halfway up into the air.

"This is precious." I couldn't take my eyes away from the picture.

"Thanks," he yawned.

"What time is it there? Why are you up so early?"

"Couldn't sleep. I already spent some time out on the porch swing. It made me think of you."

My heart swelled. *He was thinking about me!*

"Oh, did it?" I giggled.

"Yeah. And our front porch conversations."

"The ones where I cried uncontrollably?"

He laughed, "Yes, those. But let's not forget that I cried, too."

Oh, trust me, I remember.

"Why don't you try and get some rest? I'm sure you've got a long day ahead of you."

"I'd rather talk to you," the corner of his mouth began to turn into a smile, "But rest is probably a good idea, too."

"I need sleep as well. I can't seem to shake this jet-lag."

"Well, then, I guess it's good night for you?"

I nodded." And good morning to you," I smiled.

"Talk to you soon," he waved.

"Bye," I waved back and ended the call.

You're a good friend, James Moore. A very good friend.

After I had been home for about a week, Carter and I were talking in the living room while watching *The Lion King*, one of our old childhood favorites, on Friday afternoon before Mom and Dad got home from work. I was sitting in Dad's recliner, and Carter was sitting on the couch.

"So, have you decided exactly when you will be able to go back?"

"Well, I get my casts off in a week and a half, and then I will have four weeks of pretty heavy therapy. The doctor said I should be able to go back in a month and a half, maybe two, depending on the results from more blood tests, but those should be fine. I've been on top of my antibiotics. I emailed Rob and Amber and told them yesterday."

"That stinks. You must miss it terribly," I said, and then muffled under my breath, "I know I do."

"Chrissy, you loved it there, didn't you?"

"I really did. It felt like home."

"It tends to do that to you." I got up and sat down beside him on the couch, and just took a deep breath.

"I need to go back."

"I never thought that I would hear that come out of your mouth," he said.

"Neither did I," I said with a smile.

"Well, sadly you can't hop on a plane tomorrow, but there's always next summer."

"That's certainly something to think about," I said grinning.

"I don't think that requires much thinking there, sis."

"True." With this we turned our attention back to *The Lion King*, and until it was over there were no more words spoken. We had resolved my little problem.

I rolled over in bed the next morning awoken by the sound of my computer beeping from the other side of the room. I slid my glasses on and pulled my hair up as I walked over to the computer. Amber wanted to Skype! Even after just talking to James the night before, I was thrilled to be able to see another glimpse of Uganda.

"Hey Amber!" I said groggily.

"Chrissy! How are you?"

"I'm great, a little tired at the moment, but I'm so glad that I get to talk to you. How are you guys? Did you get my email?"

"We're doing great, Dru and Asher are doing very well, so are the kids. We are definitely going to do another clinic project later on. We've been so busy, that's why I haven't responded to your email. Cheryl and Stephen are still living with us, but they have found a place close to us that they are looking at. How's Carter?"

"He's doing really well, not in too much pain anymore."

"That's good, we could really use his help. It's been pretty crazy around here."

"I haven't told my parents yet, but I'm praying about coming back next summer."

"No way! Chrissy, that's awesome. We would love to have you back!"

"Carter and I were talking today, actually, and I was just telling him how badly I missed it there. I really fell in love with Uganda and all of its people. Carter just said, *'Hey, it's a summer. You should totally go back.'* Honestly, I didn't hesitate on saying yes!"

"Chrissy, that's amazing. You really have changed a lot since you first landed on Ugandan soil."

"Oh, trust me, I know. I kinda shocked myself. Everyone is acting like I'm a totally different person."

"You really are Chrissy, I can see the difference between you at the beginning of the trip and now. It's incredible. God moved in your life."

If I've changed so much over the last two months...what kind of person was I beforehand?

247

"I'm assuming that's a good thing."

"Very good. Well I better go get dinner ready, Paige is coming over to discuss future plans for Sole Hope and the orphanage. Tell Carter that we are praying for him. Love you girl."

"Love you too, tell Rob I said hi!"

"I will, talk to you soon."

"Bye!"

Carly and I ended up having another sister sleepover that night. We had stayed up late talking, and I had finally finished telling her all of my stories. In the middle of the night, my mind was spinning as I talked to myself in my sleep.

"Ava, Ava," I could see her dark curls, her deep brown eyes, it was only a dream, at the same time, it wasn't. She was there, I could see her.

"Chrissy?" Carly said groggily, shaking me awake.

"What?"

"Who are you talking to?"

"Huh, oh no one. Yeah, no one."

"Oh, okay," she said, rolling over and then whispered, "That was weird."

The next morning, I opened my journal and wrote,

Thursday, July 26th

Well, I'm home. But this surely doesn't feel like home. This house and this city and the people I hung out with before Uganda don't feel like home anymore. It's a weird feeling, really. I can't tell you how much I want to be back. I'm even dreaming of Ava. I've talked to Carter, and I definitely want to go back next summer, but I feel like that's not all I want to do. Not all that I need to do. I don't know what I need to do or where I need to be. But I do know I have the tools to do miraculous things—through Him who gives me strength.

Chapter 23

The days were growing shorter until Carter would return to Uganda and when I would go back to school.

I returned to school for my senior year and I felt like a complete stranger to everyone. They were talking about New York, the shows, the shops, everything. And what was I thinking about? My feet covered in Ugandan dirt...the smiles on the children's faces when you held them tight...Ava, and her deep, dark brown eyes...what God had done in my life over that summer.

A few weeks later, after another blood test came back clear and several weeks of therapy, we drove Carter to the airport to finally return to our beloved Uganda after a crazy summer none of us had expected.

"I love you, Chrissy," he said holding me tight, as he stood up on his own, which was a miracle in itself.

"I love you, too. I wish I could go with you."

"I am so proud of you."

"I wouldn't be at this place today without you. Thank you." He kissed my forehead. Tears dripped down my face as he walked to his plane, my heart ached with longing to go with him. I was jealous that he was going back and I was stuck here at school. He was one of my best friends. He understood me better than my own mother. And I was going to miss him more than words could say. What happened in that summer was more than I could have ever imagined.

The next day before school, I opened my journal one last time, and a note fell out on to the rug on my bedroom floor. Carter. *Here I go again. I am such a cry baby.*

I am so thankful for what has happened this past summer - even the car wreck. What God has done in your heart is something no one else can ever do. I am so proud to call you my sister...

I don't know where Christ is calling you or what he is telling you to do, but it will come- in its own time, in God's time. So for now be patient and listen to God and what He has to say.

"For I know the plans I have for you' declares the LORD, 'Plans to prosper you and not to harm you, plans to give you a hope and a future." Jeremiah 29:11

Hold fast to God's promises. And wait for His answer- because His timing will be impeccable. "For I know the plans I have for you." He knows Chrissy- He knows...

Acknowledgements

What an incredible journey this has been. This moment feels surreal, typing the last words of this precious story, finishing the formatting to send off to the publishers. I wouldn't have made it to this point without many people.

I'll start off with my family. You guys are awesome. You're the best, most crazy family anyone could ask for. I love the continual singing we do around our house and the encouragement that's always coming my way for my writing. William, I love your heart for others. You are an amazing brother and friend. J-man, you always make me laugh and help me not to take life so seriously. I love you guys. Sonia Grace, you are the best little sister. When we brought you home from Rwanda, the Lord sparked a fire in me for orphans for which I am so thankful. Mom, you're the best in-house editor anyone could ask for. Dad, thank you for always encouraging me to pursue my dreams no matter how out of reach they may seem to other people. I will always be your little girl.

Where would I even be without my grandparents? Nana, Pawpy, Mimaw, and Paw-Paw there are no words to express how much I love you. I am forever grateful to the four of you for the spiritual heritage that you all have passed down to me. I love spending time with each of you and I am so thankful for all that you have invested in me. Thank you for always believing in me!

I would also like to thank Amanda, Nick, Harper, and sweet McKinley Land. I'm so very thankful for the role of family you guys play in my life. To my precious Harper and McKinley- you light up the saddest of days with those beautiful smiles. I love all of you.

Thanks to "Trentos" and Sydney. The closer we've gotten the more thankful I am for the big-brother role Trent has played in my life. In October they move to Brazil- just like Carter moved to Uganda- I can't help but smile at how things play out in my life as they have in this story I have crafted.

During the summer of 2013, my best friend and I had the opportunity to travel to Uganda with Sole Hope. It was incredible. So a big thanks to Sole Hope for all they have done to inspire this story and for the work they are doing in the lives of the people of Uganda. I can't wait to come back and visit.

I have to offer a huge thanks to my editor, Molly. I am so thankful that the Lord allowed us to cross paths. You helped me turn this book into something I am beyond proud of, so thank you. I will forever be grateful for all that you taught me.

Thank you to all of you who financially supported me in this journey of publishing. You all have encouraged me in every step of this journey. I couldn't have done it without each and every one of you.

I want to thank Melissa Trogdon. We really got to know each other after Paige passed away. You have been a great source of support and encouragement for me. I'm so glad she let me, a 16 year old, crash her life and be her friend. You bring joy to my life. I have to give a shout out to her precious girl, Haley and her niece Megan. You both are fabulous. Thanks for being so great.

I want Paige Elizabeth to know that this book is for her. Because without her, I don't know that I would be the same Bailey B. In fact, I know I wouldn't be the same Bailey B. Thank you for loving me. When I wrote to you about this book, you made me promise you a signed copy, and somehow you're still going to get it. I love you.

Thanks to Courtney Shore, Caroline and Jenna Garner. You three have been my writing assistants. You've encouraged me daily and kept me going with your smiles and comments like, "You, my friend, can WRITE!" Courtney, you've read everything I've ever written. I'd say you're my biggest fan (aside from my mother) and I'm beyond thankful for you.

I want to thank Emily Grace, my best friend for sixteen years and counting. I don't know where in the world I would be without her. She made a reader out of me, and without reading I wouldn't be much of a writer! I love you sweet friend, thanks for all the adventures we've had together and all that is to come.

Lastly, I thank my Savior. The only One I live for and the One I hope people see in me. He is the one who has gotten me through this life. He's been with me through it all and He will never let me down. His love is what keeps me going and I'm so thankful for that.

Thank you to all of those I have mentioned and to all of those who I haven't, because if I listed everyone, it would take forever! I can't even describe how much I appreciate each and every one of you. I thank God for all of you, and am so blessed He has put you in my life.

Made in the USA
Charleston, SC
06 January 2015